# Mills & Boon Classics

A chance to read and collect some of the best-loved novels from Mills & Boon—the world's largest publisher of romantic fiction.

Every month, four titles by favourite Mills & Boon authors will be re-published in the *Classics* series.

A list of other titles in the *Classics* series can be found at the end of this book.

# Violet Winspear

# PALACE OF THE POMEGRANATE

MILLS & BOON LIMITED
LONDON · TORONTO

First published 1974
Australian copyright 1980
Philippine copyright 1980
This edition 1980

© Violet Winspear 1974

ISBN 0 263 73422 6

Set in 10/10½ pt. Linotype Plantin

*Made and printed in Great Britain by
Richard Clay (The Chaucer Press) Ltd,
Bungay, Suffolk*

# CHAPTER ONE

THE ballroom was bright with chandeliers and nearly everyone was dancing, and engrossingly interested in Lord Wilde
and his young bride of a few months. It was being said
covertly that he was taking her into the Persian desert on this
trip to the legendary lost garden of Sheba in order to let the
heat, the sandflies, and the lack of fresh water rid him of the
wife he had married for the large dowry provided by her
grandfather, Jonas Tillerton, the 'toffee king' as he was
called by the people of Manchester.

The gossip was rife at the Ambassador's white-stoned
residence in Reza Shahr, where this great annual charity
ball was being held, that it would suit Tony Wilde to be free
again, but rich enough to take up where he had left off with a
well-known society beauty who adored titles so long as their
owners had plenty of money to spend on her.

Grace Tillerton, heiress to the fortune earned by the Tillerton toffee factories, had been an easy way for the impover-
ished Tony Wilde to secure an easy living. Old Jonas
Tillerton had always sworn that he would live to see a title
in the family, so as soon as Grace had completed her education he had set about securing a titled husband for her.

'She's still a virgin, of course!' Mrs. Landon St. John
fiercely whispered the words into the ear of her companion
among the gilded chairs, where the older ladies sat and enjoyed their glasses of punch and their tittle-tattle. 'Her maid
confided to my maid, who naturally told me, that she'd
never yet seen them in bed together. Well, look at the girl!
Anyone with a sharp pair of eyes can see that she's still as
she was on the day she wed that scoundrel. It's a well-known
fact that he prefers fillies who have been up and down the
course a few times and who know the tricks of the game.
That innocent child is no more than a pawn in *his* game, and
it's a sheer scandal that old Tillerton should have handed

her over to Wilde. Played on her sense of gratitude, I'll be bound. He took charge of her when his son and daughter-in-law were drowned in that cruising ship disaster — they had left her at home with a nurse as luck would have it — and after being looked after by him all those years the girl probably thought it her duty to do as the old man wished when it came to this marriage arrangement. Jonas Tillerton is a famous tyrant. She might even have been infatuated by Wilde. He's quite good-looking — takes after his mother, that actress who inveigled his father into marriage and then spent all his money — and he knows how to turn on the charm when he really wants something.'

'How long have they been married?' The recipient of all this information lifted her eyeglasses to study young Lady Wilde. 'I must say she looks remarkably young, and just a little haughty, as if she might resent curiosity about herself.'

'She probably does resent it,' said Mrs. Landon St. John, with the air of a socially well-placed, well-travelled woman who knew everyone and everything about them, including their sleeping habits. 'She has style, for all her youth. I believe that school she went to was the same one attended by Princess Irene of Greece.'

Grace Wilde wore a dress of white silk, so simply designed and so effective against the pale smoothness of her skin, the deep blue of her eyes, and her hair that was shiny gold as champagne, looped back from her brow and held in blue-jewelled pins. Her eyes were grave even when she was smiling, and her mouth was so shaped that it was both innocently inviting and slightly scornful.

No one knew, as she did, that on her wedding night she had suddenly rejected the man whom she had coolly and dutifully married. 'You damned little nun!' he had flung the words at her. 'Keep your precious virtue! There's not much pleasure to be had from a reluctant wife, only pleas instead of please!' He had flung on his robe and stormed into the adjoining room, slamming the door hard enough to wake every other person on the same floor of the hotel.

Those who thought Grace a virgin bride were quite correct in their summation. She had been married exactly three months, and the only pleasure she had out of her marriage was that her husband never touched her, or came near her, or demanded that she be a wife in anything but name. The only pleasure she had in view was this trip into the desert. She meant to enjoy it, and she closed her ears to the advice of well-meaning friends who thought she was unwise to go searching for Sheba's lost garden with a man who never bothered to hide his lack of love for her.

She was refreshing herself with an iced cordial when a young officer approached and asked her to dance with him. She smiled politely, set aside her glass and entered his arms as coolly as a petal slipped between the pages of an unread book. His eyes studied her profile and they had circled the floor a couple of times before he dared to say what was on his mind.

'Lady Wilde?'

'Yes, Captain?'

'There's no one more attractive than you at the ball tonight, yet not once has your husband danced with you.'

'They say, Captain, that the man who dances with his own wife is either a bad dancer who won't inflict himself on other women, or a man passionately devoted. We all know, don't we, that I'm the granddaughter of a toffee merchant who married a man for his title – or words to that effect. It must be diverting for the European population of Reza Shahr to have such a couple as Tony and myself to gossip about. Such a pity we're leaving in the morning to set out on our trip into the desert. You'll miss your little debates, won't you? Only a short while ago I heard my marriage referred to as a marriage of inconvenience.'

At these words his arm gripped her a little tighter. 'If you were my wife—'

'But I'm not, Captain Thorpe.' She looked up at him, then, and there was a smile on her slightly scornful mouth. 'I am married, but I am curiously my own mistress. An arrangement which I rather like, as a matter of fact.'

'You say that – almost defiantly,' he argued, for he was a lean and good-looking man, successful on the polo field and in the arms of lonely ladies. 'Do you really believe it?'

'I nearly always speak my mind, Captain, and that's why men find me disconcerting. It's true I was taught that to be devious was to be devouringly desirable, but I prefer to lay all my cards on the table. In that way I leave no one in doubt of my hand, meaning that I never cheat.'

'But your husband does, milady.'

'Has there,' she inquired, 'ever been a man who loved with a single hunger, wanting no one else but his wife? I doubt it.' The music ceased and she withdrew from his arms where an arabesqued archway led into the palm gardens. She gazed beyond the arch in an absent way, and then almost abruptly she walked out of the ballroom into the moonlight that shone through the arching fronds of the tall palms. She breathed deeply of the night air, redolent of the flowers that kept their petals folded during the heat of the eastern day, only to unclose them when the sun went down and the soft darkness came, bringing with it a refreshing coolness.

'If you're going to stroll in the gardens, then you should have a wrap.' Captain Thorpe detained her with his hand, and instantly she knocked it away as it had been a scorpion. The look she turned on him was impatient and cold as ice.

'I'm perfectly all right and don't need to wrap up like a hothouse orchid afraid of a breeze. I love the feel of its coolness almost as much as I enjoy the sun during the day. I come of Manchester stock, Captain. I'm no wilting flower, you know. My grandfather is one of the most feared and hardened men in the north. In some ways I take after him.'

'You?' The young soldier looked incredulous. 'You have all those women in there beat for looks and pride, don't you know it? You could have any man you set those dark blue eyes on – dark sapphire eyes.'

'How absurd!' She gave a laugh and walked among the oleanders that hung their huge heads beside a meandering

8

path through the garden; their scent was strange, almost more bitter than sweet, as if giving warning that poison lurked in their rising sap. Grace touched them as she passed by them and they felt soft and firm as velvet, like the sands out of which they grew. 'If you're going to talk that kind of nonsense, then I would prefer you to leave me alone, Captain. I like my own company, so it will be no hardship.'

'You look so charming, and yet you can be so cruel.' He gave a rueful laugh and continued to walk beside her. 'I begin to think that Tony deserves a little sympathy. It can't be easy for any man to be married to a snow maiden.'

'By all means sympathize with my husband,' she rejoined. 'I've never asked anyone to feel sorry for me because I let myself be part of a loveless match to please an old man. We all, at some time in our lives, do a foolish thing out of a sense of obligation, or affection. I allowed Tony to make a titled lady of me, but I will allow no man to make a plaything of me. Do you understand?'

'Absolutely, and I respect you for it, oddly enough. So in the morning, Lady Wilde, you're off to the sandy wilds to search for the garden where Sheba was said to have made love with Solomon. Do you believe you'll find it? The legend is that those who find the garden also find love. Are you hopeful of finding the love rather than the garden?'

'With my husband, do you mean?' She turned in the moonlight to look at Michael Thorpe, and her face was pale, shadowed by a drooping palm frond which waved in the night breeze and partly masked her face.

'Would it be so unusual for a young wife to want the love of her husband? You have an air of coolness, but I believe you have a warm heart. I can't imagine that you like to hear the gossip about him? The linking of his name with that of—'

'Please don't say it,' she broke in. 'I quite like you, Captain, but it wouldn't break my heart to lose your friendship.

'You're loyal to him, eh?'

'As you are loyal to your regiment, because you took an

oath to be so.'

'Such duty can sometimes be – dangerous.'

'Are you warning me not to take my desert trip? Then you warn in vain, Michael. I wouldn't give it up for anything. It's the one thing Tony has given me which I really want.'

'People are saying—'

'Yes, what are people saying? That I look frail and might not survive the rigours of the desert. The heat by day, and the coldness that falls over the desert at night, and the fact that travellers sometimes have to drink at old wells and run the risk of infection? I'm not a fool. I know all this for myself, and I would take the risk alone just to see the real desert and not the tourist part which surrounds this gracious old residence. It wouldn't merely satisfy me, to take a few snaps of the sunset and the nomads that pass by. I want to be a nomad for a while, come what may. It will make such a change from being a dutiful granddaughter, and an unloved wife.'

'You say it so calmly.' Michael Thorpe stared at her as she stood there in the moonlit garden of this house on the edge of the desert, her white-clad, slim and youthful figure tense with longing for what lay in the heart of the desert.

'Happiness is the most elusive thing on earth to find and grasp,' she said quietly, while in the jasmine hedges nearby the cicadas made their husky night music. 'I was never like other children, you know. I lost my parents when I was a baby, and my grandfather had little use for a girl child beyond having her taught all the right things, so that one day she would be suitably equipped to become the wife of someone like Tony. I suppose I could have rebelled when Grandpa told me that Tony Wilde was going to come and woo me. I had heard about him. I knew that he was well-born, gay and irresponsible, and being only twenty I still believed that romance was a possibility. Then I met Tony and I allowed his good looks to blind me to his reputation as a Lothario. I had a duty of gratitude towards my grandfather and so I allowed myself to be talked into a marriage which I knew would never be a truly happy one. Whatever my life now is, I've helped to bring it up upon myself, and it would be childish of me to blame everything upon Tony. There are even times when I quite like his company. He rides well, and is a superb swimmer, and there have been times when we have enjoyed each other's company. As a friend—'

Grace broke off and caught her breath on a sigh. 'I shouldn't be telling you all this. I can only be boring you. Why don't you return to the ballroom and find someone more receptive to your charm, Captain? I'm merely a rather disillusioned married woman whose entire heart is only set on enjoying an expedition into the desert. There are girls in there who'll give you a far better time than I can.'

'But I like to listen to you.' He leaned against a palm tree and took a cigar case from his pocket. 'Do you mind if I smoke, Grace?'

'Please go ahead,' she said at once. 'I learned very early from my grandfather to enjoy the aroma of a good cigar.'

'I think you also learned from him that men are basically out to please themselves.' A match flared against the cigar and the aromatic smoke filled the air, mingling with the scent of jasmine. It always struck Grace as brave and tenacious of the starry white flowers to bloom so abundantly in a climate that was so brutal at times. She knew that everyone regarded her as a fool to be taking on a trip that would bring her into contact with the hot, harsh realities of the desert. But she was a girl without the promise of married happiness, and she was in the mood to challenge fate.

'Are you pleasing yourself at the moment, Captain, or are you merely trying to please me by offering your company and your sympathy?' she asked, with her slightly ironic smile. She knew that to all outward appearances she seemed to have most of the things desired by women. Good looks, a flair for dressing well and having enough money to buy the most luscious fabrics, and above all she could go wherever she chose and not be bound by family ties. Her grandfather had his business clubs and his cronies, and he had never been a man to desire feminine company. Her husband had affairs of his own to enjoy, so he didn't really mind if she flirted with good-looking officers. She did sometimes wonder what his reaction would be if she took a lover, and flaunted him, and didn't care who knew of the affair. She suspected that the Wilde temper would flare and Michael Thorpe's words would be proved very true – that men liked to please themselves, but they didn't really consider that women had the right to indulge their longings and desires. They were chattels, whichever way the situation was looked at. It was bred in female bones to be dutiful, and men took advantage of this all along the line.

Grace thought of the nights when after the dances and the parties were over she was left alone with Tony. She didn't dare to think of what she would do if he should ever insist on making love to her. She didn't hate him. She wasn't physically revolted by him, yet she knew that to be forced to submit to a man she didn't love would drive her to the edge of real despair.

She had spoken the truth when she had said that she took after her grandfather in certain ways. He had been ruthless enough to make a fortune for himself, and that strain of ruthlessness was tucked away in the graceful body of his granddaughter. She knew that if driven to it, she would hate with a fierceness that would even frighten a man as boundlessly sure of himself as Tony. She sometimes wondered if his reason for leaving her alone lay in his instinctive awareness that it was safer to have an indifferent wife than one who actively hated him.

'It strikes me as strange,' said Michael Thorpe, 'that a girl as attractive as yourself should be so uncertain of a man's sympathy. It gives me pleasure to be with you in a palm garden, even though I know that if I should attempt to put my arms around you, you would probably scratch out my eyes.'

She gave a slight laugh. 'I shouldn't go as far as that – with you, Captain. But I should turn on my heel and go inside the house.'

'Do you know,' his own laugh was a little wry, 'I'm not sure that I'm flattered that you wouldn't go for my eyes if I kissed you. It strikes me as a bit indifferent that you would merely march off back to the ball.'

'It at least proves that I wouldn't want to do you an injury,' she rejoined. 'I don't like to hurt my friends.'

'When you refer to me as a friend, you leave me no hope at all that I shall ever be – your lover.'

'Any man who hopes for that is placing himself at the call of a lost cause.' She spoke very firmly. 'Just because I happen to be an unloved wife it doesn't mean that I'm panting to become someone's mistress. I'm really rather a cool-natured person. I can live without all the overrated passion which everyone talks about—' And then she bit her lip, for she knew that she had given away to Michael Thorpe the intimate fact that she and Tony were not lovers. She tilted her chin as she saw the gleam that came into the Captain's eyes.

'I'm going in,' she said, moving away from the lean, uniformed figure. 'Tony and I are setting out early in the morning, and it's about time we returned to our hotel.'

'Grace, I hate to see you unhappy!'

'But I'm not.' She gave him a quick look. 'There's more to life than love. It's a very much talked about emotion, and yet whichever way I look I see women having affairs, or gambling. And men chasing every likely prospect for sex without a bit of real feeling attached to it. I don't much like the world at the moment, and that's why I'm leaving it behind for a while to breathe the clean, free air of the desert. It might be a savage place, but at least it isn't as uncivilized as our so-called modern society. That society strikes me as a jungle, but out there in the desert everything is so open – so free and gold and blue. I don't doubt that it can be a cruel place, but people can be far more cruel!'

'There are people in the desert, Grace, and not all of them are kind.'

'Oh, don't tell me you're about to trot out that old chestnut about hot-natured nomads?' She laughed, and for the

13

first time that evening her laughter rang with youthful zest. 'Mrs. Ladon St. John took it upon herself to give me dire warning of these men who have an overwhelming desire for every female they catch sight of. As Tony is a first-rate shot, I'm sure I shall be quite safe when this lustful nomad swoops out of the blue to snatch me away to his black tent. I can't imagine even my uninterested husband standing calmly by to watch the kidnapping of his wife.'

'Some of these desert people are lawless, and many of them are crack shots. I should know, because I've sometimes come up against them in the course of military duty.'

'Meaning?' She gave the young officer a challenging look.

'There are those who are dangerous, Lady Wilde. As you so correctly say, the desert is a vast place, where many things can happen and not be discovered for a long time afterwards. You could be carried off and the bones of your husband left to go dry and white in the hot sun before they are found, and it's too late to help any woman who falls into the hands of someone with no scruples with regard to a pretty woman. You're pretty, Grace Wilde, young and fair, unhappy and a little reckless at the present time. What would you do if what seems so improbable as we talk in this garden within sound of dance music and sight of the Ambassador's guard should ever become very probable and you found yourself at the mercy of a merciless man? Compared to some of these men who live by the laws of the desert your own husband is almost a saint, and you with your bright hair and your lovely white skin would appear like an angel to some marauding nomad with the hot lust of the desert running strong in his veins.'

'You paint a vivid picture, Captain. I don't doubt for a moment that desert men can sometimes be dangerous, but no expedition without some danger attached can be exciting, and Tony and I will not be entirely alone in that vast sea of sand. We shall have our guides and our baggage men; our cook, and tent servants, and a couple of men to take care of the horses. We shall be quite a small expedition, and Tony has made sure that each man selected is good at his job, which means that they are also capable of handling firearms. Tony isn't a fool because he likes to dance and play around. He's widely travelled and he knows how to take care of himself.'

'Does he know how to take care of you, Lady Wilde?' Emotion reasserted itself in Michael Thorpe's voice and he took a sudden quick step forward and blocked the path back into the lighted residence. 'Does he truly care that nothing should happen to you? Some people are saying – gossip is implying that it would suit him if something happened to you. There's a woman back in London whom he knew very well before his marriage to you – an experienced courtesan type, whom his type prefers to a girl of innocence. You know all this! Better than we who only guess at the truth. Look, why not take a friend along on this trip? I could get leave—'

'No, Michael.' She touched his arm, and her smile was strangely sweet. 'You're kind, but I have to face up to what life holds in store for me. I went into this marriage with my eyes wide open, and I'm not afraid of going with Tony into the desert. Some people would say that I'm being wise in keeping him apart from his – courtesan. Who knows? If we find the garden of Sheba together, we may yet find some sort of happiness together.'

'You're too good for him!' Michael crushed out his cigar against the trunk of a palm tree, as if he needed to do something violent to relieve his feelings. He tossed away the half-smoked cigar, and then before Grace could stop him, he caught at her hand and carried it to his lips. He kissed it forcibly, letting her feel the heat of his lips and the edge of his teeth.

'If I were a desert mercenary I would carry you off right now,' he said, holding her hand pressed to his jaw. 'If I wasn't so damned British, so well trained, so stupidly gallant, I'd throw you to the grass, make you mine, and make it impossible for Wilde to do anything else but divorce you. I believe in my heart that it's the only way for you to find

15

happiness, to be forced into a relationship with another man. Your own sense of duty forbids you to give yourself voluntarily to anyone else. You took vows of honour and you won't dishonour them. You're a lovely person, Grace Wilde, but also a foolishly gallant one.'

'Perhaps.' She drew her hand free of his. 'Perhaps it is gallantry, but then again it might be sheer dogged obstinacy inherited from Jonas Tillerton. Having taken on a Wilde man, perhaps I hope to tame him. And now I'll bid you good night, Captain. Don't follow me into the ballroom. Stay here and don't get talked about. Too many eyes have been on Tony and myself tonight.'

Quietly, with the gracefulness which made her name so appropriate, Grace walked away from the lean young officer without looking back. The breeze that blew through the garden was laden with a mixture of scents, and she knew the scent of the desert to be among them, distilled over the many miles into a beckoning fragrance which she could not ignore.

What she intended to ignore was the whisper that her danger lay in Tony not in the desert itself. She neither loved him nor was loved by him, but she didn't want to believe that he planned her destruction out there in the golden sea of sands.

# CHAPTER TWO

THEY had been back at the hotel for about an hour, and Grace had changed into a cinnamon velvet robe with graceful hanging sleeves, and her hair was unbound and free on her shoulders. She had checked her baggage for the following day, and the sight of the things she was taking with her on the trip had awakened her sense of excitement and dispelled that faint apprehension which the words of Michael Thorpe had aroused.

Her fingers stroked the corded material of her riding breeches, the fine linen of the pink shirt she would wear with them, and the knee-high, wine-coloured suede boots she had been unable to resist when she had caught sight of them in that little shop during her tour of Reza Shahr.

This wasn't the first time she had been to the East, for she had done a world tour with her grandfather when she was nineteen. They had visited lots of places, but none more intriguing than a palace at Shiraz in which they had stayed as the guests of one of Jonas's many surprising acquaintances. It had been an enjoyable holiday and for the first time she had hoped that her grandfather meant to make a real companion of her.

She recalled the lovely inner courts of the palace, and the various people she had met. She had been allowed into the *harem*, which had been forbidden to Jonas, and she had been highly intrigued by the number of women which a wealthy Persian still kept for his comfort and pleasure. She had learned some of the secrets of Eastern allurement, and how to cook a cous-cous. She had also been a guest at the wedding of the *agha*'s ninth daughter to the son of a great desert dynasty. There had been many guests at the wedding, which had lasted three days and three nights.

Grace still remembered a feature of it which had so fascinated her at the time and lingered in her memory. She had gone into the great hall to see the bride in her heavy brocade dress and her crown of real jewels, seated like an idol on a high-backed chair while everyone paid homage to her finery and her good fortune in securing a rich bridegroom – a man she had never seen until the moment of their marriage.

The heat and the noise had finally sent Grace to one of the courtyards in search of some fresh air and a little solitude, and there, as she sat on the tiled rim of a fountain, amid a cluster of heavy white lilies, she had heard a man singing in the depths of the garden, an aria from *La Forza del Destino*, a favourite tenor aria of hers.

For a long time afterwards she had enjoyed the experience in retrospect, for the voice had been as superbly sure of itself as any she had heard at the Opera House in Manchester, with the Italian lyrics perfectly expressed and with a seducing lilt to them, as if the singer truly believed in the forces of destiny. And being a Persian he would believe in fate – *kismet* – the hand reaching out from nowhere to lead a person to heaven or purgatory.

Grace felt certain he had been Persian, for she had not seen any Europeans at the wedding apart from Jonas and herself. She took him for one of the hired entertainers, or maybe a friend of the groom, who had arrived at the wedding with a small cavalry of friends all riding sleek horses and clad in embroidered shirts, dark cloaks and turbans of various colours. When she had rejoined her grandfather inside the palace Grace had studied the men with their dark, aquiline faces and fiercely amused eyes that a mere girl should stand among them with her eminent grandparent and seem totally without the shyness or the sex-awareness of their own women. She had wondered which one of them was the owner of the fine tenor voice, but whoever it was had not sung again, but it was that experience at Shiraz which made the prospect of a desert journey less unnerving for Grace than it might have been for a young woman who had not mingled with eastern people at one of their weddings and heard at midnight of the third day the firing of the palace cannon to announce that the marriage had been successfully

18

consummated.

She wandered on to the balcony of her hotel bedroom and leaning on the iron balustrade she thought of her own marriage in a lovely old church on the Wilde estate, which her grandfather's wealth had saved from the auctioneer's hammer. She had worn white velvet and a cap of pearls, and she had carried dragon-petalled lilies. Jonas had wished her to carry orange blossom, but she had rebelled against this wish. Romance was attached to orange blossom, and she had known from her first meeting with Tony that like that Persian girl her marriage had been arranged, a dowry had changed hands, and she was to be no more than a bride of convenience.

The moon that still rode high in the sky struck its light across her face, and made it easy for her to study the gold ring on the third finger of her left hand. The ring had lain on the white velvet prayer-book, such a gleaming symbol, but for them it had represented a loveless match; a binding of two people with no real bonds to hold them fast together. The words of the marriage service came stealing back to her: 'With this ring I thee wed, with my body I thee worship.'

But not in her company, nor in that of anyone else, did Tony assume *la masque d'amour* just to pretend that he cared. He seemed to derive an odd satisfaction out of showing people that she meant very little to him. Perhaps it was his revenge for knowing he did not possess her body.

She gave a little shiver, and was turning to go back into her room when she seemed to catch sight of a movement in the grounds below her balcony. She leaned over and a breeze stirred against her bared neck as her hair swung away from her face. A great palm tree branched up close to her balcony, and the thought crossed her mind that a thief could easily climb it and gain access to her room. At the ball tonight she had been wearing the pearls which had been a wedding gift from her grandfather; they were rather famous, having belonged many years ago to a Venetian lady whose jealous husband had strangled her with them. It had amused Jonas to tell her the story when he had placed them around her neck. It was as if he had been telling her that Tony Wilde would never be aroused to such jealousy, arising from over-riding love, and she need have no fear of the pearls being used again in a rage of passion.

But they were worth a lot of money, and she scanned the moon-shadowed grounds in an attempt to catch sight of a stealthy, robed figure. There was no one. All was silent but for the moon-fooled cicadas, and the shifting of the palm fronds in that intermittent breeze.

Grace frowned, for her little show of nerves revealed that she was not undisturbed by her conversation with Captain Thorpe. She had dismissed Mrs. Landon St. John's talk of ardent, unscrupulous *khans* as a lot of novelesque nonsense, but she did know, better than Michael Thorpe, that Tony had reason to want her out of his way. She knew all about Chandra Lennox, the woman in London, beautiful and mercenary; sensual and destructive to even the happiness of women with faithful husbands. If Chandra wanted something, then she set out to take it, and she didn't care at all if a wife stood in her way. She had the fatal charm of the born seductress, and Grace knew very well that her own husband was a willing victim on the altar of Chandra's greed.

Then Grace frowned, for Michael had implied that *she* was the victim and that if she didn't take care she would not return from this journey into the desert.

It was at that precise moment that she heard Tony enter her bedroom from the adjoining room. As always he had taken the best, most luxurious suite in the hotel, so that to her relief they had separate rooms in which to sleep during their stay at Reza Shahr. For their desert trip he had bought large single tents, but as always when he entered a room of hers she tensed and wondered if he meant to insist on becoming a husband in more than name.

'What are you doing out there?' He strolled to where the louvred doors were opened on to the balcony. He wore a dark red dressing-robe of Turkish silk, with a cream cravat at his throat. His light hair was sleek against his skull, and his eyes as they ran over her were half taunting and half admiring. He had never concealed the fact that he thought her attractive; he had once said that he wouldn't have married her, despite the Tillerton Tons, if she had been sallow and thin, with a bad skin. He liked, he said, other men to be envious of what he owned, and she would be amazed how envious other men could be of a fellow's good-looking wife, his title, his two racing cars, and his stable.

'I'm glad,' she had rejoined cynically, 'that you put me before the horses, at least.'

Tony had laughed, and then he had said: 'You're a sport, old girl, but what a pity you're also a bit of a prude.'

And now as she looked at him from her moonlit balcony she assumed the cool, remote look which he termed her look of prudery. It was a better safeguard than anything else, for Tony's vanity required that a woman should desire him, and the cool blueness of Grace's eyes had long since convinced him that she was a frozen statue of a girl without any natural feelings.

'The moonlight suits you,' he drawled. 'It blends with that icy purity of yours. I sometimes have the feeling that you prefer the elemental things to human beings; those stars up there, and that great yellow moon, and the night moths that flit about your hair as if attracted to its fairness. At the ball tonight you didn't look quite mortal. I believe some of those fellows were afraid to approach you until Thorpe dared all for the regiment and saved you from being a wallflower. I can never make out, Grace, whether you're shy, or just damned unnatural.'

'Would you prefer a wife without virtue, Tony?' She couldn't help but speak coldly as she thought of Chandra Lennox, who certainly lacked virtue.

'It would be nice to have a wife who was a little more human – or should I say less goddess-like.' His eyes flicked her from head to toe, taking in the cinnamon velvet that contrasted so well with her pale skin and her hair that was almost ashen by moonlight. 'Perhaps I should make another attempt to bring you down to earth, my dear Grace. It might make a world of difference to you to be brought to your knees, a plea for mercy on those cool and lovely lips that I suspect have never been kissed. You really are the epitome of the wife in name only, and I must be a fool for allowing such a farcical situation to go on. Tomorrow we go into the desert. Perhaps all that golden sun will melt some of the ice from around your heart, and you and I—'

'I'm tired, Tony.' She swept past him into her room. 'I don't wish to talk about what may or may not happen on this trip of ours. Let it be enough for now that we're going there – together.'

'Looking forward to it, old girl?' He followed her into her bedroom, and she felt his gaze flicking the turned-back bed-covers, and moving to her riding-kit laid out on the ottoman at the foot of the bed. She saw a smile quirk at the edge of his lips. It always amused him when she wore her boyish riding coat and breeches, and invariably tucked her hair under a brimmed hat. She had not a voluptuous figure and could almost pass for a boy ... a very good-looking one, with lashes a trifle too long around the straight blue gaze that she gave to everyone.

She gave him that straight look right now. 'Are you looking forward to it?' she asked. 'You won't be bored after a day or two, with only your wife for company?'

'As I just intimated, my dear, there are always compensations for a married couple, if you will only learn to accept life with a little more *savoir faire* and a little less intensity. Love, whichever way you look at it, is only a game to be enjoyed.'

'I thought it had something to do with honour and integrity.' Grace looked cool and haughty as she spoke, but inwardly she was rather disturbed by the trend of the conversation and by the way her husband was looking at her. In a manner of speaking he had right on his side. She denied him what he had the right to expect from a wife, and she glimpsed in his eyes a smouldering impatience which might flare into actual danger once they were on their own in the desert, miles from the people with whom they had attended the ball tonight. For the first time she felt a little afraid of Tony Wilde, but she shrugged it off and went to open the door that led into the adjoining room.

'Good night, Tony. It's late and we have to start early in the morning. I understand that Captain Thorpe and a few of the other officers are riding with us as far as the plain, and we don't want to be sound asleep when they arrive to see us off.'

Tony strolled towards her, sleek and well-groomed, and faintly mocking. 'Thorpe has a bit of a crush on you, eh? It was his idea that these fellows form a sort of guard of honour. Does he know you're as cool as Mont Blanc, or did you show him another side to your nature? I'm sure there has to be one, as you're the granddaughter of a man who pulled himself out of a slummy back street by the straps of his hobnailed boots. That took nerve, and a passion for the good things of life, so don't make out you're all grace and virtue.'

So saying he walked into his own room, and Grace firmly closed the door behind him. She could feel colour high on her cheekbones, and she knew her eyes were blazing. If there was one thing Tony was sure of it was that she would never cheat on this marriage of theirs, but she knew it gave him a sort of pleasure to accuse her of cheating. It excused some of his own misbehaviour, and made him feel a little better about enjoying the money that now flowed into his pockets from her grandfather's factories.

She stared at the door that stood closed between them, and she was strongly tempted to turn the key that jutted in the lock. But if she did so he would hear the key being turned, and he would know that he had shaken her composure.

She walked to her bed and untied the sash of her robe. As it slid from her shoulders she gave a little shiver, as if something touched her, and as she slipped into bed she recalled that moment when she had thought a figure had flitted beneath her balcony. Usually her nerves were very steady ones, and once again she blamed Michael Thorpe for disturbing her with his frank remarks.

She turned out the bedside lamp and slid down beneath the covers and the netting which saved anyone with a fair skin from being bitten in the night by anything winged or legged which might enter from the tropical gardens.

She lay absorbing the silence, and frowned a little as she remembered that her Venetian pearls still lay as she had left them on the dressing table, glistening there amid her toiletries, with the ruby clasp somehow symbolic of the crime of passion to which the pearls had lent themselves. Worn as a single rope the pearls reached almost to her knees, so she bound them in three rows about her neck, and sometimes wore them as a belt around a certain blue dress of which she was fond. It wasn't usual for her to be nervous of things, or of people, but tonight, despite the fact that she was tired, it took her some time to fall off to sleep.

Morning dawned with a promising blaze of sunshine, and immediately she awoke Grace was out of bed and into the bathroom, where she took a cool shower and then liberally sprinked herself with cologne. It would be hot riding in the desert and Grace didn't want to spoil her enjoyment of the ride by feeling tacky. She combed cologne into her hair and then French-pleated it so it lay cool off her neck, with two soft waves just above her temples.

She returned to her room, where she slipped into the minimum of underwear before dressing herself in her tailored silk shirt, light-weight breeches, and soft, wine-coloured boots. She then checked that she had loaded her small pearl-handled automatic – just in case – and secured about her left wrist the small gold watch that was her only jewellery today apart from her wedding ring. The lovely pearls, with their strange history and their innocent lustre, she locked away in her jewel-box, which was then placed in the pigskin suitcase which would be taken down by a porter to join the rest of the luggage.

Grace took a last look round her hotel room before leaving it to go and have breakfast with her husband. She caught up her brimmed hat from the dressing table and approved her own cool and workmanlike reflection in the mirror. During the days that lay ahead of her she would dress like this, presenting almost a boy-like appearance as she rode beside Tony across the desert sands. In her luggage there were dresses for evening wear, the cool and simple sort that not only suited her personality but were just right for wearing under the desert stars, when the hot sun had died away and camp had been pitched for the night.

Michael Thorpe had asked her if she intended to search for Sheba's lost garden in the hope of finding a little happiness with her husband. Here in the daylight, an hour before setting out on that search, she gazed into her own eyes and saw there a certain little shadow. Did she hope – did she really believe that she and Tony could find some sort of happiness together?

At that moment her door was thrust open and Tony looked in on her. 'Are you all set, old girl?' he asked. 'I'm ravenous for breakfast, and we'd better eat hearty because camp won't be set up much before noon, when it will be necessary to rest from the midday sun. Come along, wake up! You look just about ready to leap on-stage as Peter Pan, and I will say if a woman has to dress like a boy it's all to the good if she has your type of figure. These nomad chappies like their girls voluptuous, so we won't have to fear any lust and rapine.'

'Do shut up!' Grace strode towards him in her long suede boots, a short riding whip in her hand. 'Your mind seems to run on the same lines all day long. Women are people, not objects to be lusted after all the time.'

'Cool as ever, eh?' He lightly touched her nape, and she forced herself not to jib away from him like a filly from the jab of a spur. His touch recalled what he had said last night, that love was a game and he didn't intend to be bored in the desert.

It was still very early, so they breakfasted in comparative privacy in the hotel dining-room. Grace was deeply excited rather than hungry, but Tony wolfed a large plate of ham and eggs and drank several cups of coffee. He was wearing a light tweed jacket with his breeches, and as always his fair hair was impeccably groomed. Grace cut a peach into sections and recalled that time in Cannes when they had been mistaken for brother and sister. She smiled to herself, and Tony glanced up from his breakfast and caught the smile.

'What's amusing you?' He stared at her as the sun struck through the windows near their table and lit her hair to a shining gold colour and revealed the amusement in her blue eyes.

'I was thinking of Cannes,' she replied. 'Do you remember those people who took me for your sister?'

'How could anyone blame them, Grace, when you behave just like my sister?' There was a taunting note in his voice and a slight twist to his lips. 'In a way it rather amazes me that you're the granddaughter of old Jonas ... he isn't exactly the epitome of courtliness, yet you have all the airs and graces of a lady born. Old Mrs. Landon St. John was saying last night that I'm to be envied for having a wife who represents all that's best in British womanhood.'

Grace ate her peach and refused to rise to the taunt. She didn't want to start their trip in a bickering mood, so she changed the subject and talked instead about their luck in acquiring such excellent horses.

Their guide was a Persian who spoke excellent French, and he had taken Tony to the very best stables for the hiring of their mounts, and Tony had selected a proud bay for himself and a well-balanced, shining chestnut for Grace. The horses and their guide, Kharim, awaited them in the courtyard of the hotel. The remainder of their small caravan had set out early for the oasis where they would make their first halt.

As Grace thought of being in the real desert, with nothing but sand all around them like the rough pelt of a tiger, she felt quivers of excitement coursing through her body. When she had travelled East with her grandfather they had not camped in the desert, but even then she had longed to do so. It was as if her very soul had stirred to the idea; as if the spell had reached out then to take hold of her. It was she who had casually broached the idea to Tony, after she had read about the lost garden of Sheba in the autobiography of Rachel Leah Bourne, the woman who had spent most of her life in the East, and who had disappeared for several years, not to be heard of again until her manuscript had been found in a trunk in an old oriental house in which she had once lived. The book had been thought so interesting that members of her family in south England had agreed that it should be published. It had proved to be a best-seller, but it had not brought Rachel Leah Bourne out of hiding, and finally it had been assumed that she had died in the desert during one of her trips.

Grace hadn't dreamed that Tony would agree to them taking a desert trip . . . and looking at him in the morning sunlight she didn't want to believe that he meant her any harm.

'You're quite certain you want to go?' She dabbed at her lips with a table napkin and assumed a casual air. 'I — I could go alone, you know. It wouldn't worry me to do so.'

'Don't you believe that it would worry me?' he drawled. 'You aren't exactly anyone, old girl. You're Lady Wilde, and you have a rich grandparent. It would hardly be safe for you to travel alone.'

'So you're coming along to protect me?' She couldn't keep a cynical note out of her voice, for there was no keeping Chandra Lennox out of her thoughts. For a moment she was wildly tempted to ask him exactly what were his intentions with regard to his girl-friend. He certainly couldn't marry her while Grace was legally his wife, and a divorce would mean that he had no more access to the Tillerton thousands.

Tony looked at her, and she gazed back at him, her face a composed and lovely mask in which only the eyes were alive and intensely aware of all the dangers inherent in a marriage made for gain and not from love. Grace was young, untried, but not blind to life. She knew that people weren't angels . . . but the question was, was Tony quite a devil?

# CHAPTER THREE

THE sight of the oasis, just before sundown, had been like a miracle of green glimpsed after the long ride across those lonely stretches of golden sand and baked flats of mud where wattle grew, sometimes in gallant straggling clumps that soon withered beneath the onslaught of the desert sun.

Tony called out to their guide to make camp, and Grace was not sorry to slide from the saddle of her mount and to stretch her legs while the men set about putting up the tents and gathering brushwood for the cook fires. It was not often that she was called upon to ride such distances in the kind of heat that never really abated, but she soon found that as the sun died away in an awesome burst of colour, the dusk that quickly followed brought with it a breeze that was welcome and yet curiously cold after the warmth. She had been warned that the desert was a place of extremes, that its sun was hot and its nights were cool.

She watched as the tents were raised, and saw the brushwood flames leap around the sides of the coffee pot as it was placed on the fire; the beans were roasted on the flat of a shovel and would be ground and dropped into the bubbling water to emit an aroma so enticing that it made the memory of drawing-room coffee seem very tame.

Her husband came over to her, having given orders which would secure comfort for both of them in the form of plenty of hot water for a wash, and then a meal together in his tent. 'After which,' he drawled, 'we can play cards or look at the stars. These people say that everyone's destiny is written in the stars, though how on earth one reads them is a mystery to me. Well, my Grace, what do you think of your first day in the desert? Personally speaking I shan't be sorry to have a soak in that folding bath of mine – just think, old girl, some of those nomads we passed a few miles back never touch water except to drink it. They rub themselves down with sand, I'm told, and that's why their skin has that burnished look. Did you notice those women? Barbaric as the Queen of Sheba herself, with the same animal insolence, I'll be bound. They had silver and jewelled bangles on their ankles, did you notice?'

'Yes,' said Grace. 'Even in the wilds women have an instinct for self-adornment, and the ankles are really all they reveal beneath those long *djellabas*.'

'They're a strange people,' Tony murmured, leaning his back against a palm trunk and lighting a cigarette; a brand specially blended for him and with a tiny gold coronet stamped into them. 'A Moslem is permitted four wives and he can divorce them for the slightest annoyance. Once, twice, thrice, begone, he says, and the little woman trots off.'

'Taking her dowry with her,' Grace could not resist adding. She felt the look which Tony shot at her, his eyes narrowed against the smoke of his cigarette. 'All the goods and chattels she brings with her she takes away again, for Eastern law isn't that cruel or simple. You forget, Tony, that I travelled with my grandfather just after I left finishing school, and we stayed with some Persian friends of his, and while we were there a wedding took place. I visited the *harem* to watch the wedding henna being applied to the bride's hands and feet – lovely lacy patterns – and I was told that although the girl is betrothed to the man when very young, her parents safeguard her against his future repudiation by making it part of the marriage contract that if he should find her unpleasing and wish to annul the marriage, then all the gifts contained in the dowry would return with her to her father's house. Those silver and jewelled anklets you saw on those nomad women are her safeguard against divorce. While she has them, and her husband can call upon her to pay debts or buy sheep with them, then she's safe against his temper or his dissatisfaction with her.'

A short and telling silence followed Grace's words, and then Tony gave her a glittery smile under the thin sweep of his moustache. 'Warning me not to play the devil with you, Grace? It's an empty threat, if so. I made sure that old Jonas made over that money in my name.'

'I know exactly what you did to acquire it,' she rejoined, and her own smile was cool as ice. 'I was merely thinking that in some ways, although the nomad woman appears to have a hard life, she's really far more free to be herself than I am. As Lady Wilde I have to play the role of good sport, even to the extent of not appearing to care that you married me for money, and I married you because it gave my grandfather a kick to see his granddaughter driving away in a wedding car with a coronet on the door. You and I, Tony, have reaped what we sowed, have we not?'

With these words Grace walked to her tent and after entering it she firmly closed the flap behind her. The oil lamps had been lit and she glanced round with satisfaction. The folding bath was open, ready for the hot water, and a big bath-towel had been laid out ready for her. Her suitcase stood on a stool, from which she would select a dress for the evening, and the camp-bed was made up. All in all it was a comfortable tent, and she gave a smile as she tossed off her slouch hat, then took off her long boots.

Ah, that felt better! She ruffled her hair, and proceeded to take from her case the things she could need; her silk pyjamas and her toiletries, not to mention her simple, lovely lingerie which had been made for her by the Sisters of the Bleeding Heart, a convent at home where she sometimes went to visit a friend with whom she had attended school, and who had renounced the outside world for that of an enclosed order of nuns.

Grace fingered the soft silk of a slip and wondered if she could have had the courage to give up so many of the worldly things that were truly enjoyable. The wearing of nice clothes, or the exchanging of them for the dark grey habit. Dancing and riding, and travelling. Grace bit her lip. It was because her grandfather had taught her to like and appreciate all these things that she had allowed him to persuade her that marriage with Tony would be fun, if not the high romance that young girls dreamed about, and in a sense she had taken it on as a challenge, just as her friend had taken vows of poverty, obedience and chastity.

She tensed as a hand touched the flap of her tent, but it was one of the servants bringing the hot water for her bath in the great copper kettles, which he tipped into the tub, not saying anything but with that look in the dense eyes which accepted all *roumia* as slightly crazy. With a *salaam* he withdrew, and Grace proceeded to undress for her bath and to hope that one of those silent-footed men wouldn't suddenly reappear as she sat soaking herself.

After that long ride it felt so good to relax in warm, scented water, but all the same she didn't linger too long, for she felt hungry and she wanted after dinner to take a walk to the sand-dunes that rose like ramparts beyond the palm trees of the oasis. Soon the moon would be up and the scene would be a breathtaking one.

She quickly towelled herself down, cooled her skin with cologne, and slipped into her lingerie. The dress she chose to wear was of champagne silk edged at the wide sleeves with softest mink fur. She clipped her hair away from her brow, and applied make-up very lightly. Outside the tent she could hear Tony giving orders about their meal; even here in the desert he expected the best of food, and wine to go with it.

Grace flicked aside the tent flap and almost at once she felt the coolness in the air, blowing towards the oasis where they were camped, across the many miles of empty desert. Grace decided that she was going to be cold without a cloak, so she fetched the scarlet *burnous* which she had bought in the *suk* at Reza Shahr, and swung it about her slender figure as she walked towards the folding table which had been laid for their evening meal, complete with silver cutlery and stemmed wine glasses. She couldn't resist a smile, and at the same time she took a deep, luxuriant breath of the wonderful, untainted air.

The tall, leaning palms etched their shapes against the starry sky, and beyond them lay the sandy range that curved high and then rolled down into long vistas of sheerest solitude. Grace stood there, her eyes shining by the light of the million stars on the surface of the sands. The beauty of the night thrilled her, and in a way it also frightened her, for so much of it was unknown as yet. In her every fibre she felt aware of every small sound, the barest flicker of a palm leaf, the changing shadows as the men moved about the camp fires, attending to the food, and talking together in low, guttural voices. Her face, had she known it, looked hauntingly lovely by the blaze of the pagan stars.

She knew with even more intensity that she had longed for all this for a long time now; yearned to be away from all the bright lights and chatter of the life which Tony chose to lead. Whatever his motive in bringing her here, she was glad she had agreed to come.

She turned to him with a smile, and he indicated the laid table with a sweep of his hand. 'Be seated, milady. And what will your pleasure be – a glass of champagne?'

'That would be nice, Tony, to celebrate our venture into the desert.' The scarlet *burnous* rustled silkily about her as she took her seat at the table, and she was pleased to see that fresh melon had been brought on the trip and was served in halves to commence their meal. Tony unwound the foil from the champagne bottle and removed the cork with the skill of the confirmed lover of the wine. He came round to Grace's side and filled the tulip bowl of her glass, then he returned to his own seat and did the same for himself.

'You proposed a toast to our venture into the desert, Grace.' He raised his glass and gazed intently at her across the table, lit by candles in small hurricane holders, for a spell of calm in the desert was no real indication that a stormy wind would not suddenly arise. 'Tell me, my dear, what do you hope our visit to Sheba's lost garden – if we find it – will do for us? Induce us to fall in love?'

'This is excellent champagne,' she said in a cool voice. 'I've now reached the stage, Tony, when I believe that you and I have forfeited the right to love – if there is such a thing. Perhaps all I ask of Sheba's garden – if we find it – is the assurance that not all dreams and legends are things of mist without any substance.'

'To think,' drawled Tony, spooning his melon, 'that the granddaughter of a toffee merchant should be so high-minded. Would Jonas approve of your airy-fairy dreams, d'you think?'

'Not for one moment,' she replied. 'Jonas has always been good to me, but he never really cared to know what sort of a person I was; he was only concerned that I should be fairly presentable, well-schooled, and good-mannered. With these qualifications I was bound to be a good bargain in the slave-market that passes for marriage.'

Tony drank his champagne and gave her a droll look. 'You sit there looking as if ice wouldn't melt in your mouth, but you're quite a rebel on the quiet, aren't you, my Grace? You really fire up over certain things and a man sees in you something to really ignite his imagination. So your estimation of marriage is that it's a form of slavery, eh?'

'Is it anything else?' she asked quietly.

'I can't recall, my sweet, when I ever made a slave of you.' Tony gave a laugh and added more champagne to his glass. 'Anyone would think that like a desert *khan* I kept you in a *harem*, but instead you have freedom to explore the desert on horseback, to say whatever you please to your indulgent husband, and to dress as if this were a Paris nightclub instead of an oasis.'

The scarlet cloak had fallen away from her throat, and her skin and hair were very pale in the glow of the candles. She knew as she was served lamb cutlets and vegetables that the robed servant flicked his dark eyes over her, but she also knew that it was curiosity rather than anything else that induced these men of the desert to look at her. They obviously found her very different from their own tawny-skinned women, whose hair was like night rather than sunlight.

'I felt like a change of dress after being in breeches and kneeboots all day,' she said. 'You're wearing evening clothes yourself, so what's the difference? These men probably think we're a couple of crazy Europeans, so what does it matter if it amuses them to see us sitting here like this? Did

33

you imagine I would hide myself away in my tent and eat alone as nomadic women do?'

'I somehow didn't expect you to dress yourself up – oh, not that I mind, Grace. I'm all for being civilized, so long as you realize that we're now among people who are still a bit primitive. In breeches and long boots, with your hair covered, you look quite boyish. But tonight you've emerged in your true colours, and that tall guide of ours, that one who calls himself Kharim, has looked at you more than once in the past hour. He's standing over there by one of the fires and I've only just noticed how tall the fellow is, and how black and sinister he looks with that beard.'

Grace followed the direction of Tony's eyes, and she saw the firelight leaping its red light over the dark, hawk-like face of their guide as he stood, a cloak flung back from his shoulder, drinking coffee from a smoky mug. His beard was clipped about the line of his jaw and densely black, and above it jutted a commanding nose, and above that a very alert pair of eyes shaded by dark eyebrows with an almost Mephisphelean slant to them. Grace had already noticed that in the saddle he was extremely upright, but a supple rider rather than a stiff one. Like desert men he gave an impression of having been almost born in the saddle, and he knew good horses, for it was he who had advised Tony on which horses to select for this trip. She had an idea it was he who had selected the horse she had been riding all day, a sleek, well-bred creature, mettlesome but easy enough for a good rider to handle, and Grace was a good rider.

As she gazed at this man who was to guide them many miles across the sands of Persia, she thought to herself that he had the look of a leader. There was aggression in his stance, and in the way his shoulders held that cloak. He knew he was under observation by his employers, yet he neither looked at them, nor gave any sign that previous to Tony's remark he had been studying Grace.

Up until this moment she had noticed the man without really studying him, but now she decided that he looked rather overbearing, as if he were giving his services rather

34

than being paid for them.

'Did you say he was educated?' she asked Tony. 'He looks entirely haughty to me and has a superior air of being in charge of a pair of half-grown children. After all,' her voice rose and she said something which normally would not have entered her head, 'he's only a paid servant like the other men.'

Her clear English voice carried beyond their table and Grace knew that their guide would have had to be deaf not to have caught her remark. She was at once ashamed of it, but chose to be defiant about it, and turning in her chair she called out to Kharim: 'Would you mind adding some more wood to that fire, as you're just standing about doing very little.'

At once his eyes flashed to her, and she had an immediate feeling that the eyes of a Persian leopard would flash like that only seconds before it leapt upon its prey and tore it to pieces. Grace could be foolish in her pride, but she could also be gallant and she gave back to the man a cool look of daring, the play of the candle flames over face, the scarlet *burnous* draped lightly about her shoulders so that her gown and her pearls had a frame for their expensiveness.

He stared at her with the most unnerving intensity, and then with an indolent bow he moved from the fire and gathering brushwood from the pile that had been gathered from the edge of the oasis, where the hot sun had dried it, he flung it on to the fire until the sparks leapt high and seemed to smoulder in his eyes. Then he swung on his heel and strode out of sight. Grace continued with her dinner, and though she should have felt a sense of elation because she had made the man bow to her will, she felt instead a strange chill of fear. He was, after all, in charge of this expedition and they were in his hands, here in the desert, far from their friend the Ambassador at Reza Shahr. He might be Tony Wilde's employee, but he had the power to make life pleasant or unpleasant for two Europeans who had no idea in which direction lay the next waterhole, or the next oasis where a stream usually fed the trees and provided shelter

35

from the intensity of the sun.

'These fellows don't enjoy being ordered about by a woman,' Tony drawled. 'You'd better leave me to give the orders, Grace. We can't afford to antagonize anyone as important as our guide — I understand that it lowers their prestige if they do a woman's bidding.'

'It's easy enough to see that he has a high opinion of himself,' Grace rejoined. 'And I don't doubt that he considers women as inferior objects. Well, he's free to think what he likes of his own sort of women, but he isn't going to treat me as if I'm part of the baggage. He could see that fire was sinking and yet he stood there drinking coffee as if he were the master and here to be waited on. No wonder Michael told me to watch out for the arrogance of these desert men!'

'Michael?' Her husband tautened in his chair and gave her a sharp look.

'Captain Michael Thorpe, who saved me from being a wallflower at the Ambassador's ball.' She said it drily, and added sugar to the coffee which had just been poured for her. She turned her chair towards the desert and her nostrils tautened to the mingling aromas of desert air, coffee and woodsmoke. The whispering of the leagues of sand mingled with the rustling of the pendant palm leaves, and overhead the moon was rising, huge and golden as a pagan shield. The stars were fading in that golden light, and the distant sands were patched with immense velvety shadows where the hillocks rose and crested, tipped with moonlight. The beauty of everything was awesome, and as Grace sipped her coffee, excitement ran through her veins.

The desert dream was real at last and here she was, drinking dark, smoky coffee beside a camp fire, while the horses wandered about in their compound, and the robed staff moved among the tents and the piles of baggage and harness.

Tony rose from his chair and came to stand beside her with his own coffee. 'So you got as far as calling him Michael,' he grunted. 'It came to my ears that he was a pretty fast worker with the ladies, and we all know that the ladies have a weak spot for a uniform.'

'Really?' She gave a laugh and rose from her chair to walk where a palm tree towered. 'Don't tell me you're feeling a twinge of jealousy on my account?'

'I have that right, whether you like it or not.' Tony followed her. 'You're my wife, and I won't have the Wilde name played about with.'

'I can hardly play about with it here in the middle of the Persian desert,' she pointed out. 'If I were that type, I'd have stayed behind at Reza Shahr while you wandered, and enjoyed Michael Thorpe's company without any restrictions.'

'Then why didn't you?' he growled. 'He looked your type – tall, gallant and moonstruck.'

'Strange as it may seem to you, Tony, I actually find the desert far more fascinating than any man I've ever met. Haven't you said often enough yourself that I'm unnatural in my likes and dislikes? You should be glad of it in a way. It ensures that I shall look after the Wilde name and not toy with it. What a pity—' She broke off and shrugged her shoulders. 'No matter.'

'What were you going to say?' he demanded. 'What's a pity?'

'Well, Tony, you aren't exactly the most honourable guardian of your family name, are you? You're fond of pointing out that desert men hold a primitive view of women, but you believe in the double standard yourself. A wife must be above reproach, especially if her husband has a title, but it's no one's concern if the husband cares to stray. It's accepted with a benevolent shrug that he's a bit of a rogue, but heaven help his lady wife if she gets caught with her hair down.'

'Really, Grace!' Tony was making his protestation as a tall, cloaked figure appeared from out of the shadows, the clipped beard shadowing the lower part of his face.

'Lord Wilde?' The voice was deep, the words spoken with a foreign intonation that struck Grace as being like rough silk drawn over rocks. She had glanced at him before she could prevent herself, but he was looking at Tony and the

37

line of his profile had to her gaze a hawklike, almost insolent pride; a dismissal of her as anything more than a mere woman.

'What is it, Kharim?' Tony had to look up at the guide, who was a head taller than he, and with shoulders in proportion to his height. Grace sensed that her husband felt slightly unsure in the company of this man and not quite certain that he should behave with his usual air of lordly superiority. There was about the desert man a natural hauteur, but all the same it amazed Grace that her husband should lose his air of assurance in the presence of a man in his employ. A stirring of scorn mingled with her surprise . . . she thought of all the warnings she had been given about taking this trip, and she knew herself to be deep in the desert with a husband who would be no match for his Persian guide should a disagreement flare between them.

'I wish to know if you're making an early start in the morning, Lord Wilde?'

'I did plan on that. It's cool in the early morning and we can put a few miles behind us before the sun starts to burn so confoundedly—'

'I would advise against breaking camp tomorrow morning, milord.'

'You would, eh? And why, may I ask?' Tony jutted his chin as if to assert his right as master of this trip.

'I am informed by one of the porters that he can smell a storm on the way—'

'But look at that moon,' Tony objected. 'Clear as a bell! Would it not be overclouded if a sand-storm was getting ready to pounce?'

'These things give warning in the sands themselves, milord, and I never argue with men who have lived all their lives in the Persian desert. They have an instinct, an ear for the changing whispers of the sand, and I feel sure it would be unwise to break camp and to leave the oasis which offers shelter from the open desert, where trails can be swept away by the high winds, and a caravan can be lost before it can recover its bearings.'

38

Perhaps it was the note of hauteur in Kharim's voice which made Tony argue with a point of view so much wider than his own where desert weather changes were concerned. 'Don't let's get into a panic about a probable storm,' he drawled. 'That sky up there looks pretty clear to me, and if we wake in the morning to a calm day then I see no reason for hanging about here until a bit of a sand-blow hits us. My orders are that we pack our gear first thing and continue with our journey to this mythical garden in the desert which Lady Wilde is so eager to see. Tell me, Kharim, is there anything to substantiate the legend? Does the garden exist, or are we making a fool's trip?'

The guide stood there with the moonlight full on his dark, lean face, the full cloak draped with a nonchalant desert grace over one broad shoulder. All about the three of them stood the tall, faintly rustling palm trees, and his silence seemed deliberately drawn out until suddenly he looked directly at Grace, and once again she had an impression of eyes that missed nothing. Every movement of a facial muscle, every glance and every smile was noted and analysed by this man. He had the deep-set, alive and searching eyes of a lynx, and when he walked he had the noiseless spring of a leopard in his legs.

He was not a man whom Grace could like, but she felt certain he knew all there was to know about the desert and its unpredictable moods and strange legends.

'Within the garden of Allah there are many other gardens,' he said, in that deep, rough-silk voice. 'Some are gardens of roses, others are gardens of ruins. It would, perhaps, spoil anticipation for my lady if I describe for her the garden for which she searches.'

'You've seen it?' she broke in, with a curiosity stronger than the coolness she had sworn to maintain towards the man. But it was his knowledge of the desert which intrigued her; the way he spoke of the place in subtle, almost seducing terms.

Asked directly if he had actually seen the lost garden of Sheba, he spread his strong, brown, long-fingered hands.

And then once again he looked at Tony. 'It is strongly possible that a storm is on the way, milord, but you are the master, you give the orders, so it is for you to decide one way or the other. I can only say that a sandstorm in the desert is not a pleasant experience for men, let alone a woman.'

'Really?' Tony gave a careless laugh. 'I can assure you, old chap, that my wife is no wilting lily, for all that she looks as if she just strolled out of a Paris salon. She comes of tough stock, y'know. Her grandfather minted a fortune out of mint toffees, and she won't thank you for suggesting we lose half a day's travel in order to save her from getting a bit of sand in her hair. It's what she came for. She loves all this sand – this primitive wilderness. Ask her!'

But Kharim merely gave a brief bow in answer to Tony's decision to set out early in the morning regardless of the change in the weather that was brewing. He walked away, silent and lithe in the high leather boots with the thick felt soles that made walking on sand so much easier.

'He's a darned officious type,' Tony muttered, when Kharim was out of earshot. 'If I give in to him over every small issue, then he'll soon be giving *me* orders. You're right about him, Grace. He's only a paid servant and has to be shown that he is.'

'He could be right about that storm,' she said. 'It might be foolish, not masterful, to ignore that sort of warning.'

'But just look at that moon up there!' Tony pointed to it. 'Yellow as a daffodil and big as a pond. Would it shine like that if a *khamsin* were imminent? No, the fellow just wants to unnerve us, to make us feel dependent upon him. I wish now that I'd not been persuaded by him to let him be our guide. But back there at Reza Shahr he seemed less high and mighty and more reserved – but now we're out here and he thinks we're dependent on him, he's showing himself in his true colours. It's a typical Eastern gambit. These fellows are full of guile – one minute as charming as Eros, and the next as devious as the devil. No, I'll be damned if he'll tell me what I should do every minute of the day! He was hired to guide us, not to direct us!'

'Of course,' she said. 'Let's see what the morning brings. Right now I'm beat and I'm going to bed. Good night, Tony.'

Grace was walking away in the direction of her tent when her husband caught her by the arm and detained her. She turned quick eyes to his face and her own face wore a look of instant, cold rejection. 'Please let me go!' she said, keeping her voice low but meaning every word.

'You're another who's fond of giving orders.' His fingers tightened painfully on her slim arm under the cloak. 'I have every right to share that tent, if I so wish.'

'By all means share it,' she said coldly, 'but you'll sleep on the floor. The camp-beds are single ones, remember? It was you who ordered them, Tony, not I.'

'You're quick and clever with your answers, aren't you, Grace?' His eyes glittered under the angrily narrowed lids. 'But I wonder how clever you'd be if you ever came up against a man without the advantages of a European up-bringing? One who'd whisk aside your words as if they were sandflies and bring you to your knees, begging for mercy!'

'I'd never beg,' she said scornfully, 'but I might kill.'

'My dear,' he laughed, 'how melodramatic! You mustn't take seriously all that opera you were so fond of back in Manchester. What a deadly bore it was for me, taking you to the opera as part of my wooing. I might as well not have bothered, for your Mancunian grandfather had already decided on the match, had he not?'

'And you had already decided to accept the money he offered,' she rejoined. 'We both know our own weak spot, Tony, so there's no need for yet another post-mortem. Jonas can go to his clubs and talk gleefully to his cronies about Lady Wilde, his titled granddaughter; and you can enjoy life without the nuisance of getting into debt. In a way we deserve each other. I hadn't the spirit to defy a rather selfish old man, and you – you bought a bride, but I'll be darned if you'll make me as shop-soiled as some of your other – amusements!'

She pulled free of him with these words and swept towards her tent; the heavy red silk of her cloak rustling about her and expressive of the sheer disdain and anger which had boiled in her at the idea of being used as a distraction for Tony now they were together in the desert and he was far away from the sort of female company he preferred. Her eyes were blazing with her blind anger and she had walked into a tall, dark figure before she could stop herself.

'Oh!' Her hand threw itself out and met the hardness of a broad chest, her head reared back and anger, shock and moonglow met in her eyes as she saw who it was who caught at her and steadied her.

'Something has frightened you, my lady?' The question was polite enough, but the voice itself held a silken awareness of her emotional state. Hatred of her marriage flared higher and found suddenly, and irrationally, a target in this man.

'Take your hands off me!' she stormed. 'How dare you grab hold of me and question me? Who do you think you are?'

'Merely your *servant*, Lady Wilde.'

And never in her life before had Grace heard so much soft insolence in a voice, exactly like a talon sliding across silk and leaving it cut to ribbons.

She allowed her eyes to hate his dark face, surmounted by the roped headwear, and then she was free of his hands to enter her tent where she pulled the flap closely into place, and then stood in the lamplight, unmoving for several minutes, feeling as if she had passed through a storm and been bruised. Men! First Tony, with his decadent appeal to her duty as his wife . . . and then that desert nomad, that overbearing guide, with his voice that played on the nerves like a cat's talon playing with something smaller than itself!

Grace flung off her *burnous* and let it lay in a pool of scarlet on the carpet covering the floor area of the tent. She unwound her pearls until they reached to her knees . . . her hands gripped the pearly rope and she wished to heaven that when she had been left an orphan by the tragic death of her parents, she had not had a rich, covetous, demanding man like Jonas to bring her up and make her feel that she owed him some return for her education and her keep.

A shiver of tiredness ran through her, and she began to prepare for bed. She had brushed her hair and loosely braided it, and was about to turn out the lamp when she heard a movement at the tent flap and realized that she had forgotten to tie the ropes that secured it. She had spun round from the lamp, a hand at her robe, when the flap was jerked open and her husband entered. He had discarded his jacket and tie, and there was the burning fury of several glasses of brandy in his eyes. His hair was no longer smooth and Grace saw the gleam of the diamonds he loved in the ruffle of his white shirt.

The thought flared through her mind that he had all the rakish appeal of the decadent lordlings of the Regency era – but she was no trembling girl-wife of the same era, and she felt nothing but a weary disgust as she looked at Tony and caught the aroma of the cognac he had been drinking.

'I'm about to go to bed,' she said. 'What do you want?'

'You,' he said, and his insolence was crude, like the look he swept over her lightly clad figure. 'And I'm about to go to bed myself.'

'You've been drinking and you look disgusting,' she said. 'Now get out of my tent and leave me in peace. Get out!' She swept past him with these words, intending to open the flap, but he gave a supple leap, caught hold of her and spun her to face him. His eyes were furious, and then as he looked at her, hating her and desiring her at the same time, he swung his hand and hit her across the face. The sharp pain of the slap made her cry out and brought tears to the edges of her eyes. Her senses spun. Never in her life before had she been physically molested, and it was both a shock and an indignity almost beyond bearing.

'Who do you think you're talking to?' Tony gave her a push that sent her toppling to the floor, where she was saved from a bruising by the thickness of the carpet. Tony stood over her while she lay there gathering her senses and her breath. Her long braid was flung across her face, and her

43

eyes looking up at him were appalled, unbelieving, but not really frightened. She could not be frightened by someone so spoiled and selfish, who had allowed his temper to take control of him in this spiteful way.

'You frigid little cat!' He drew back his right foot, still shod in a black evening shoe, and an instant before it landed in her ribs she rolled out of his way and her hand found contact with the open suitcase at the foot of her bed. On top of the articles in the case lay her small pearl-handled automatic, and she had gripped it and raised it before Tony could come at her again with his angry feet and hands.

Grace had told Michael Thorpe that something of her grandfather was inherent in her, but he had looked sceptical, as if it were impossible that a slender and graceful girl could have anything in common with a tough and hardened Mancunian. But the blood of Jonas ran strong in Grace at this moment, and she raised the automatic a little higher, and held it in a hand that neither trembled nor wavered. Her grandfather had given it to her when they had travelled together in the East and he had taught her how to use it.

'Put that thing down,' Tony ordered. 'It'll go off in a moment!'

'It will if you touch me again.' She knelt there on the carpet, the gun directed at his startled face. 'It's typical of your basic immaturity to set about a woman, and it's shown me very clearly that we can't go on with this farce we call a marriage. It was never a marriage, but a misalliance, and the sooner we end it the better. In the morning you will inform the guide that I wish to return to Reza Shahr. What you do yourself is of no concern to me. I've had enough!'

'And what do you think I've had?' He looked belligerent, but he made no attempt to come any nearer to the pretty but deadly little weapon which she held so firmly. 'I've had no affection or comfort from you. Not a taste of the love and obedience you swore to give me.'

'You've had money and the mercenary comfort which that brings.' Her voice had the clear ring of crystal. 'And if it will take a bit more to undo this marriage, then you're welcome to what my grandfather settled on me when I came of age. All I want is to get away from you as soon as possible.'

'Thanks.' He thrust his hands into his pockets. 'You can put the gun away, Grace. I can assure you it's cooled my ardour—'

'Do you usually demonstrate your ardour with a slap round the face?' she asked scornfully.

'You try a man's temper, Grace, with your cool indifference. Well, no one can say you aren't a chip off the old block – you're positively made of marble, heart and body, and I hope to heaven you meet your match one of these days. Some man whose feelings *you* won't be able to penetrate.' He turned away from her and flung over his shoulder: 'About that settlement? Are you serious?'

'Never more so.'

'Right. Then we'll discuss it tomorrow – on the way back to Reza Shahr.'

He left her tent and as the flap fell into place she seemed to breathe the tang of a strong cheroot. Then everything was quiet again and her grip on the little gun relaxed. She stared and stared at the oriental pattern of the carpet. Her cheek still stung from the weight of Tony's hand, and her heart was achingly rebellious. Jonas would be so angry with her decision to divorce Tony that she hardly dared contemplate the fight that lay ahead of her. But it was a fight that was inevitable. She and Tony were hopelessly ill-matched, and heading for real trouble unless they separated.

She gave a sigh, secured the fastenings of her tent, and climbed into bed. The little gun she pushed beneath her pillow, and as she fell asleep she seemed to breathe again that tang of foreign tobacco, strong and faintly aromatic. As sleep overcame her the thought just brushed her mind that Kharim the guide might be strolling about on his rounds of the camp before settling down for the night himself.

Had he heard them quarrelling? The question followed her into the realms of sleep, and all about the encampment the sands whispered, while the moon overhead blazed with a sort of mist over its face.

# CHAPTER FOUR

GRACE was awake as early as dawn, and soon she had washed herself in the cold water left in the ewer, and dressed herself in a shirt and breeches. She shook out her long boots to make sure a scorpion had not crawled into them during the night and after she had pulled them on she went outside her tent.

The darkness of night had slipped away and the sky was lighting up. A breath of coldness stole through the oasis and the tall palms had a melancholy air as they stood in silence against the grey sky. Their long leaves shone with dew, and the smell of the desert was indescribably fresh, and the dunes seen through the trees had the stillness of a scene painted on canvas.

Grace could not suppress a sigh, for in her heart she knew that she longed to stay in the desert, to continue this journey, but she could no longer face the thought of continuing it in the company of Tony. She put her hand to her cheek and knew that he had left a bruise on the cheekbone just below her eye. She had powdered her face and could only hope that the sharp eyes of Kharim and his staff would not notice it. It was somehow cheap and humiliating to be the victim of a physical attack by her husband; it wasn't as if Tony felt any true passion for her, all he wanted was to break her spirit, to tarnish her pride, and she hated him for that and could no longer endure his company.

She stood lost in her thoughts for about twenty minutes, and in that time the camp began to come alive and the aroma of woodsmoke drifted to her nostrils as the men began to light the fires for coffee and breakfast. The last tinges of darkness had fled away, but the morning was still strangely grey so that the sands had a spectral look. The sun seemed reluctant to break through the gauze of dawn, to rape the virgin coolness and threaten the day with passionate heat.

It was instinct rather than sound which made Grace aware that someone had approached and was standing nearby. Each nerve in her body rang a warning of further conflict, but when she swung round it wasn't her husband who stood looking at her but the guide. 'Good morning, my lady,' he said. 'An oasis is a peaceful place, but may I suggest that you cover your arms. The air when slightly damp brings out the mosquitoes from the palm trees and their bite can be unpleasant for anyone with so fair a skin.'

'It's all right,' she said moodily, 'as we're not going on with our trip but will be heading back for Reza Shahr, you need not fear a fevered woman on your hands in the desert. If you have not yet seen my husband, you can rest assured that his orders are the same as mine. The trip is cancelled, but you and your men will be paid the full amount as agreed upon. And, Kharim, please don't ask me any questions!'

'It is not the place of a servant to do so, my lady.' His tone of voice was smooth, but when his gaze dwelt directly on the bruised side of her face Grace knew that he had heard her fighting with Tony the night before. The guide knew she had been struck, but being a man of the desert he wouldn't regard such treatment as so very terrible. She felt sure he was more tough than tender in his dealings with his own women, and she tilted her chin and looked icily proud when she saw his lip curling, there in the black shadow of his clipped beard.

'I hope we can expect to be back at Reza Shahr by evening fall?' she said. 'The weather seems calm enough this morning.'

'Have you not heard of the calm before the storm, Lady Wilde?' And as he raised his glance to the sky Grace for the first time caught a glimpse of the colour of his eyes; always before they had been partly concealed by his rather heavy eyelids and the density of his lashes. It startled her to see that his eyes were green as jade; a striking, water-clear jade. She was staring at him when those eyes flashed again to her face, and at once she dropped her gaze to the upstanding collar of his cloak, the folds swinging back to reveal his hard

47

brown throat. There was a barbaric quality to this man's looks ... such a man couldn't be expected to sympathize with a woman who wished to change the plans of an entire expedition because her husband slapped her.

'We shall just have to take a chance on the weather,' she said. 'No doubt you think me fickle, and probably spoiled, but I have no need to explain my actions. You and your men will not lose by this change of plan and you will probably be glad to see the last of us.' Grace shrugged her shoulders. 'I shall have some coffee before I pack my belongings.'

As she spoke she walked away towards the encampment, where the table had been set up and where Tony was lounging, smoking his morning cigarette. 'You were up with the lark,' he said, and his gaze slid off her face as if a stab of shame attacked him. 'Not that I can hear any larks. Rustam, that chap who waits on us, is the one who predicts a sandstorm. D'you think we ought to hang about here just in case it hits us? Perhaps it wouldn't be wise to hurry away—?'

'Do whatever you please,' she said. 'I've made up my mind to go back to Reza Shahr and I shall take one of the men as porter and guide if you decide to stay here.'

'Can't you wait to get back to the gallant soldier boy?' Tony spoke in a voice that carried beyond their table, and Grace was certain that Kharim heard him, for she was convinced that the guide understood English, though he never spoke anything but French. She knew also that Tony was vindictive enough to want to make her look the typical spoiled and capricious European woman. She must take the blame for this change of plan. She must be made to look the type of wife who deserved to be slapped. Her deep blue eyes gazed directly at Tony, letting him know that he could no longer hurt or humiliate her. Their marriage was over and all she wanted was to be free of his presence as soon as possible.

Rustam poured the coffee, then brought bacon, fried eggs and toast to the table. Grace could feel the man looking at her, wanting to speak, to offer warning of what the sands threatened. She bent her head to her plate and was relieved when he walked quietly away. From the corner of her eye she saw him approach the tall figure of the guide. They spoke together and the emphatic shrug of Kharim's shoulders indicated that he was not responsible if the two crazy Europeans wished to venture into the face of a storm.

'Old Jonas is going to be damned annoyed about all this brouhaha.' Tony's knife stabbed at the food on his plate. 'Thorpe may have a few medals, but he hasn't a title, and the old man isn't going to be pleased about that. Look, Grace, let's forget about last night. I promise it won't happen again, and you know full well your cool manner has a way of riling a man and driving him to extremes. I'm only human—'

'And so am I,' she broke in. 'And the very thought of spending a life with you is enough to sicken me. I even begin to believe the rumours—' She shrugged, for what did it matter any more what Tony had planned or hoped would happen to her during their sojourn in the desert? 'It's all over, Tony. You can't hurt me now, and neither can Jonas appeal any more to my sense of duty. I have my own life to live.'

'With the gallant and good-looking Captain?' Tony drawled sarcastically.

Grace didn't even bother to answer him, and rising from the table she went to her tent to pack away her things. An hour later the tents were down and the baggage was loaded for the return journey to Reza Shahr. Grace, clad now in her riding jacket and slouch hat, fed sugar to her horse and climbed easily into his saddle. The down-pulled brim of her hat shaded her face and gave her a pensive look, and as she fondled the satiny neck of her horse she watched the men mounting up. Tony was slouching in the saddle and looking round at the broken camp with a sullen expression on his face.

Although the sun had risen above the arching fronds of the palm trees, it had a leaden quality, like smoked metal, and there could no longer be any doubt in anyone's mind that a bad change of weather was threatening. Grace knew

49

that Tony was on edge despite his bluster about letting everyone see who was the master. He didn't want to leave the oasis, but he hadn't the moral courage to leap from his horse right now and order everyone to remain here until it was safe to venture into the open desert. Grace gave a shiver of intense dislike; she despised Tony for his cowardly arrogance, for the way he was scowling across at her, silently demanding that she call off the trek before it started.

She did nothing of the sort ... it gave her a sense of power and pleasure to canter her horse to the edge of the oasis, where Kharim was waiting to give the signal to start.

'What are we waiting for?' Grace called out to him.

He turned in his saddle to look at her, but she could not tell from his face what his thoughts were. She could only guess that he thought her a reckless little fool, and as their mutual antagonism met and clashed, it was as if the storm came alive in the air. He gave a signal with his hand, and the small caravan moved out of the oasis with a jingling of harness. Grace followed the raking grey horse which Kharim rode, away from the shade of the trees into the metallic gleam of the sun, which mated with the sand to produce a layer of heat that would be scorching in a couple of hours. This was the *Dasht-i-Sheb*, a rambling sea of yellow sand and islands of baked mud on which lay the shadows of weirdly grown sandstone, rising into the shapes of turrets and brazen crags. Across the mudflats flew black partridge and snipe, and the sullen colour of the sun gave to the scene a threatening sort of beauty. In the far distance lay a chain of blue mountains, rising above the plain like immense castles empty of humanity.

After a few miles Grace could feel the heat rising in little puffs from the ground, visible stirrings, fine wafts of sand like smoke about the legs of the horses. As she rode and watched she began to realize that a hot wind was pawing at the sands and creating that effect of smoke. Her pulses quickened, and in that instant the guide turned again in his saddle to ensure that the caravan was keeping up with him, taut and lithe in his robes, with a gaze as hard as iron.

He called out something and when the words reached her they were ominous. 'The sand dust is rising off the surface of the desert. I think the storm is coming towards us.'

Her fingers tightened on the reins of her mount and she urged him forward until she was beside Kharim. 'Can't we head away from it?' she asked. 'Isn't it possible to avoid the full force of it?'

'No.' He spoke decisively. 'We must stay on the direct route and hope it will be short and not too violent. We are a small caravan, Lady Wilde, compared to the enormous ones which have been lost when the known trails have been wiped out by the savage paws of a sandstorm. These winds can lift the large rocks that often mark a trail and carry them yards away, and I would sooner stay on a route known to me than chance another in the hope of avoiding the storm. I doubt if we would avoid it. A sandstorm is not like an English cloudburst; it is a sheer, blinding blanket of sand, driven over the plain like a tidal wave.'

His eyes, cruel green as emeralds in the lurid light stealing over the desert, stared into hers. 'Does it please you, my lady, to have played goddess with the lives of a dozen men?'

'How dare you—?' Because she was now afraid for the men she half-raised her whip as if to strike Kharim for saying she had purposely played with their lives. Her eyes blazed back into his, filled with temper and a certain torment. The livid light stealing over the sands was reflected by her skin, which seemed blanched of all colour except for the lurid mark of the bruise implanted by her husband.

'Hit me,' he said, his voice low and cutting, 'and I shall be forced to add to your bruises, milady. The mark of a man's hand is not as pretty as pearls against your white skin, and I would further add that a display of temper will only increase your sense of heat when the scorching wind hits us.'

Grace's whip-hand dropped to her side, and it was mortifying that she had to accept such remarks from a Persian guide because she had no defence in the shape of a husband

51

who cared for her. Kharim knew that Tony had marked her face, and a shudder of humiliation ran all through her slim, proud body.

They rode on into the hot puffs of air, as if somewhere in the heart of the desert a dragon had stirred awake and was casting his breath at the travellers, waiting for them to ride into his lair before letting loose his terrible fire.

Grace glanced over her shoulder and she saw that Tony had pulled a muslin *shesh* over the peaked cap which he wore. He looked a trifle absurd, and when he caught her gaze he scowled beneath the *shesh* and Grace felt as if a barb of sheer hatred flew at her from Tony's eyes. All his life he had had his own way; now he was being forced to go her way ... because of greed, and the need to get his hands on as much of the Tillerton money as he could before divorce from her closed the till. It was all so mercenary and horrible that Grace was almost glad that she was forcing him to face the coming storm. He hated discomfort of any kind, and surely the storm would be no more than an hour or so of hot wind lashing sand at them, making life a misery for a while, but not endangering their lives.

She glanced again at Kharim and saw that his profile was stern, unyielding of any sympathy, sculptured as if from tawny sandstone, the nose jutting with a fierce pride above the dark, clipped beard.

She didn't want to believe that they were truly in danger and she gave a slight toss of her head, as if in scorn of his grim look. At once she felt the flick of his dense green eyes ... leopard eyes, fierce and yet subtle, and with no spark of understanding for her dilemma; her defeat in finding herself tied to a husband who felt no love for her. Kharim was a Persian, and for him a woman was an obedient slave or she was nothing. He was too primitive at heart to know or care that women needed to be loved for more than their bodies.

'You come into the desert,' he said suddenly, 'yet you know so little of its many moods. Like a woman, the desert has many sides to it. It holds danger and delight; fury and fear. We who are part of the desert know that a toss of the

52

head won't dismiss a sandstorm as if it were a sandfly. You have much to learn, milady, and it really is a pity that you are running away from the desert.'

'I'm not running away,' she denied. 'Circumstances are forcing my hand – but you – you wouldn't understand that part of it. In your desert philosophy a woman submits, whether to blows or unloving kisses. Well, I am not going to submit to such a life. I – I'd sooner be dead!'

'Don't invite such a calamity out loud or it might be granted you.' The tip of a lash seemed to snake over her skin as he spoke. 'Surely a woman of your world is not led like a hennaed lamb to the altar – or should I say slaughter?'

'If you are asking was my marriage arranged, then the answer is yes.' Grace spoke defiantly, and because she needed to defend herself against his accusation that she led them all into possible calamity by her insistence on leaving the oasis and the shelter of the rocks and trees. As she spoke she could feel her eyes aching from the glare in the sky, and she could feel her mount straining nervously at the reins in her hot, gloved hands.

'Where was your pride?' drawled the man who rode beside her. 'That you are proud is written all over you.'

'And arrogance is written all over you!' Once again Grace felt like raising her whip to this – this hired servant who acted as if he gave orders instead of taking them.

'We are all behind our faces, thank Allah.' A thread of dry humour ran through his words, but before Grace could reply to him, her gaze was caught and held by a fiery change in the sky ahead of them. An angry welt of red seemed to glow across the horizon, tinged at its edges with a haze of saffron; a menacing vista rather than a beautiful one, and even as she watched the bruised glow was spreading over the sky and tingeing the sands with its ominous shadow.

Grace caught her bottom lip between her teeth, for instinct told her that the sandstorm was preparing to spring upon them ... like a savage tiger with a lashing tail and teeth bared to bite them. The heat seemed to intensify and as a film of sweat broke over her body, Tony suddenly galloped up beside her, spitting angry words.

'Here it comes!' he snarled. 'I hope you're happy, Grace, now we've left shelter behind us and have to face that holocaust here in the open desert! I hope you enjoy every moment of it!'

She glanced at him, and in that moment, as the storm glared upon them, she felt absolutely nothing for this self-indulgent rake who looked so hot, flushed and furious that he bore no resemblance to the man who had stood suavely beside her in church and vowed to love, honour and cherish her.

Because the thought of those unholy vows, made between unloving man and wife, made her feel so guilty, and so defeated, Grace flared into anger herself.

'Scared, Tony?' she taunted. 'I'd try to straighten your spine if I were you, unless you wish these Persian men to label you a woman.'

'What would you know about being a woman?' Then, raising his whiphand, he lashed out at her face. At the same instant a high and dancing sand-devil came spinning across the desert surface, which had a glow as of coals flung from a furnace. The lashing whip, the sand-devil, the shaking fury of Tony's body, all combined to unnerve his mount, which suddenly flung up on its hind legs, gave a shrill and frightened neigh, and dashed off across the hot sands into the glaring eye of the storm.

After a stunned moment Grace herself gave a little cry. She turned swiftly to face Kharim. 'We must—' The remainder of her words were carried away by the howling wind that suddenly unleashed itself upon them, and at the same time the guide's lean, swift hand caught at her reins and checked her impulse to ride after the man whom she had taunted into a retaliation which had made his horse nervously bolt.

'Non, milady!' Kharim spoke in decisive French. 'To gallop after your husband will only endanger you, and the horse Kismet will return at my signal.' His eyes burned into hers, intent as a tiger's, and reflecting the strange green

54

colour that was now dominating the painful saffron colour of the sky. 'We are going to have to protect ourselves as best we can ... and it does occur to me that you would pursue milord not from loving concern but from conscience, *hein*?'

'It would seem that you know everything!' Grit was now stinging Grace's lips, and she could feel her heart pounding with a mixture of alarm for Tony, and apprehension for the men of the caravan who were now dismounting and covering the heads of their mounts with great scarves of muslin. Bundles were pulled to the ground and blankets were pulled from them to provide cover when the sand came whipping at them fierce and hot enough to flay the skin from the face.

'Off your horse, milady!' It was a firm and direct order, and Grace knew that it had to be obeyed. As she slid from the saddle, gripping the reins tightly as her mount jibbed and shied from the sting of the sand, she heard Kharim whistle the horse which had bolted with Tony. A long, low, piercing signal that cut through the whine of the wind, once, twice, three times. Grace gripped the reins of thin leather until they almost cut into her fingers ... it struck her as terribly strange that a desert guide should have a horse from a hiring stable so trained as to respond to a signal. And he called the horse Kismet ... surely a rather fateful name!

Even as this reflection passed through her mind, a dense fog of sand descended upon them like a pall, shutting out the sky and all the surrounding landscape, and causing her a feeling of dread such as she had never experienced before in her life.

She felt blinded, stifled, and filled with an instant panic which made her want to thresh about like someone being smothered by a blanket. As she gave an uncontrollable cry, a cloak was thrown over her and a pair of strong, insistent hands dragged her into a kneeling position. 'Shield yourself as much as possible,' a voice ordered, close to her. 'Hold the cloak right over you and try to take shallow breaths of air. Don't worry if you feel suffocated ... it is better than being choked by sand.'

Grace crouched down in the shield of the cloak and was only too willing to take this advice from the man who only a short while ago had so annoyed her, not only by his manner, but by his remarks. Above her head raged the storm, intermixed with the jingling of harness as the horses shifted restlessly. The reins of her chestnut had been taken from her hand and she guessed that Kharim had secured him.

She felt the fast, uncomfortable thudding of her pulses, and the sweat streaming down her body, so that her silk shirt clung to her skin, and her breeches and boots seemed full of grit that added to the torment of these moments . . .

Moments? Oh, God, what if the storm lasted hours? What of Tony? If his mount had not responded to Kharim's signal, then Tony would still be out there in the open desert alone, lost in the whirling, choking, cut-glass sand. His fear would increase tenfold and without the guidance of Kharim, or the other Persians, he would be in grave danger of his life!

Grace's heart seemed to come into her throat, for if anything happened to Tony she would be to blame. She had angered him . . . provoked him . . . and though she felt no love for him, she did feel a natural anxiety, and a terrible sense of guilt.

She closed her eyes and prayed for his safety, but with fatal perversity the fury of the storm increased and suddenly it wasn't possible to hear anything but the raging of the wind, forcing the sand beneath the folds of the cloak so that Grace not only felt the harsh grains on her lips and eyelids but on all parts of her exposed skin. The torment was indescribable . . . like nothing she had ever imagined. All regrets associated with her marriage, and this journey, rose up to add their painful lash to that of the whipping wind and the pervasive dust and sand.

How far away seemed her grandfather's house, where she had spent her school holidays, and later had tried to be a companion to that irascible and domineering old man who all his life had directed people and made situations go the way that best pleased him.

What would he say to all this? And how angry would be his reaction when she told him that she was divorcing Tony? Oh, but Gramps had known, he must have realized that she was not in love with the man she had married out of a sense of duty and obligation. Gramps had even said to her on her wedding eve: 'Forget the fellow's past like a sensible girl. He's sown a few wild oats, but that's only natural in a man. Just enjoy yourself being Lady Wilde and queening it among those snooty society folk. Be a sport, Gracie. Let an old man enjoy his sense of triumph in having wheedled a title into the family. Lord love us, how your grandma would have relished seeing you all togged out to marry a real live lord!'

Real . . . live . . . Grace shuddered and had a premonition of disaster.

What had Michael Thorpe said: 'Gossip is implying that it would suit your husband if something happened to you in the desert.'

The dry taste of sand, the feeling that red-hot needles were being forced into her eyes, the thudding of her heart from lack of air, all added to the distress she was feeling. She didn't dare to lift the cloak from her head, for the hurricane of sand would scour the skin off her face. She strained her ears to catch a sound of that familiar half drawling, half sarcastic voice which would set at rest her fear that Tony was out there, at the mercy of something far more primitive than human emotions; human storms of passion and hate. The strange desert had let loose its demons, and all that human beings could do was submit to the scorching wind and the torturing sand until those demons had spent their anger, and respite came at last.

It seemed to Grace then that in the midst of the sand-storm she became rather light-headed, as if from lack of oxygen and an excess of anxiety that she had not, with a taunt of cowardice, sent Tony into the storm to be hurt by its fury.

Everything seemed to spin around her and she fell into a half-conscious heap, half smothered in the folds of the big cloak, and unaware of the moment when an intense silence fell over the desert, so sudden that it was like the high, humming silence left in space after a huge machine stops pounding out its thunderous noise.

As suddenly as it had arisen the sandstorm was ended, and one by one the members of the Wilde caravan began to emerge from their coverings of cloak and blanket. Only Grace lay as she had fallen, until a brown hand pulled away the cloak that covered her, carefully, like a skin, so that the sand coating its folds wouldn't fall upon her. She lay with her fair hair tumbled over her face, and didn't become fully aware of what was happening until she found herself propped against a muscular arm, with the rim of a water-bottle at her lips.

'Come, drink,' said a voice. 'It will wash some of the dust from your throat and help to revive you.'

Grace obeyed the voice and was grateful for the coolness of the water easing the constricting dryness from her throat and reviving the senses which the storm had clouded. In a few moments she was almost herself again and brushing the gritty hair from her eyes she glanced slowly up at the man who held her, his arm firm and hard about her body.

Her eyes studied the sun-darkened face, which seemed to have the strength of sculptured rock. The long brows seemed to tally with the strong length of the nose, and the clipped beard added to the man's look of ruthless authority, and the eyes set in all that darkness had a sort of radiation about them . . . green and dangerous and gem-hard.

'My husband,' she said, and the sand that had scraped her throat made her speak huskily. 'Has he – returned? Is he – safe?'

'He has not returned, milady.' Kharim's reply was direct and uncompromising. 'I have just sent three of my men to search for him. It will be a difficult search, as the storm has obscured all tracks in the vicinity, and it may take several hours before Lord Wilde is located.'

'Then he – he was alone in the storm!' Shock, and pity, registered in Grace's blue eyes. 'How awful for him! Most especially for him, for he has always been so – so pampered and protected and waited on. Such an experience will make him insanely wild—'

'If he is found unharmed, then he will surely be too grateful for his life to retaliate against you, milady.' The deep voice was impersonal, but Grace saw a narrowing of the long eyelids and a sharpening of the jade eyes. 'So you care after all for his safety, enough to fear his anger.'

At any other time Grace would have told this man to mind his own business, but right now she knew him to be in total command of her and the awful task of finding Tony. She gave a weary shake of her head. 'I don't fear Tony, or any man,' she said. 'But like any normal person I fear the elements . . . they are far more ruthless than any person could be. They attack without reason, or provocation, and I wouldn't wish my worst enemy at their mercy. When you signalled Tony's horse the wind must have carried the sound out of earshot?'

'On the contrary.' With a slight but explicit movement of his hand Kharim indicated one of the horses, a sweating, sand-covered bay with a weary, downbent head. 'The animal returned alone, milady, so your husband must have dismounted of his own accord, or been thrown from the saddle. We must hope that my men will find him, but you must appreciate that the outlook is not a highly hopeful one. The storm winds have played havoc with the surrounding landscape, the shifting sands have buried landmarks and wiped out the smallest chance of finding a foot track, a hoof-mark, leading to the spot where Lord Wilde might have attempted to take shelter . . . or where he might have been landed if the bay threw him.'

Kharim paused and that gem-hard look was back in his eyes. 'You must try not to blame us, or yourself, if the search proves abortive, Lady Wilde.'

'Please . . . don't say that!' The sandstorm had been intolerably hard to endure, shielded as she had been by Kharim's cloak. She could hardly bear to think of anyone having to suffer it all alone, scoured and battered, and perhaps buried

59

by the sand. She looked at the Persian guide for some small sign of hope, some glimmer of assurance in his eyes that Tony would be all right. But his face became in a moment a bronze mask, not exactly unkind but unwilling to raise hopes on the unpredictable desert sands. He knew those sands too well.

With a sigh Grace pulled free of his arm and rose to her feet. She was disturbed by how shaky she felt, but she tried to conceal this from Kharim's hawk eyes, and proceeded to brush the sand from her breeches, and to remove it from her hair with her small pocket comb. That strange calm which had followed the storm still brooded over the desert; the sun was lost behind clouds and so it was cooler.

Grace welcomed the coolness, but nothing could dispel her sense of calamity, which every remaining member of the caravan seemed to feel. The men stood about silently, like robed statues, gazing at the distant sands which now seemed to whisper as the wind blew across the desert.

Grace sought the face of Rustam, but it was mask-like, as if all the men had taken their cue from Kharim and would reveal no more than he did.

No one spoke and the minutes dragged by, and all at once, in a driven way, Grace made for her chestnut horse. 'I can't just stand here, waiting, thinking the worst,' she cried out. 'I have to go and look for Tony!'

She was about to take the stirrup when a pair of hands descended on her shoulders. 'No!' The word was explicit. 'My best men are out searching for your husband, milady. They will find him if he is to be found. The rest is with Allah.'

'Is that all you can say?' Grace swung round to face Kharim, and her face expressed a young, bewildered anguish. 'If anything has happened to my husband, then it's my doing! And it's my right, and my need, to join that search! How dare you give me orders to the contrary?'

'It is not a case of daring,' he said. 'I am telling you that neither you nor any more of my men will leave this spot until the others return. You think you can fight the desert, milady, but you can't. You take what comes, with as good a grace as possible.'

'Take what comes?' she cried out. 'Kismet? The will of Allah? With a fatalistic shrug of my shoulders? That is a human being out there! A man who is a stranger to your awful desert! Have you no compassion for him, or is such an emotion foreign to your nature?'

'If, Lady Wilde, you had listened to my advice and stayed at the oasis, none of this would have occurred. You placed pride before any other consideration, and you might as well know that if one of my tribesmen were out there, lost, perhaps hurt, maybe lifeless, then your suffering would be a lot worse.' In his hand his plaited whip made a slight movement that spoke volumes, and in that moment Grace became more than ever aware of this man's air of authority, his commanding stance in the robes which fell in sculptured folds about his tall figure, the way his booted feet were firmly planted in the sand.

She stood tense as the meaning of his words rushed over her. *His tribesmen. His?*

He was looking down at her, reading her eyes as they comprehended that he was more than a guide in charge of a small caravan. More than a hired servant to take orders from a woman. More to be feared than any other man she had ever met.

'Who are you?' The words broke from her lips, rushing through her like a shout and coming out in a whisper.

'I am milady's servant, hired to do her bidding, and to bow my head in submission to her demands—'

'No guide would be as insolent as you are!' That deep-down stab of fear was like a goad, prodding Grace into argument with this man who had only to snap his fingers to make other men do his bidding. She resented him, disliked the bold way he had of standing, his robed head entirely unbowed, his clipped beard very black against his bronze skin. He had none of the graceful good looks of the Persians she had met that time she had travelled East with her grandfather; his manners were arrogant rather than charming.

'What game are you playing?' She flung the words at him, and hated him with intense blue eyes. 'Why are you pretending to be a guide when you are obviously something else? It makes no sense—'

'What in life, after all, does make sense?' A black eyebrow arched above his green eyes and he seemed to be mocking her, playing with her, showing not an atom of sympathy for her plight ... that of a woman whose husband was somewhere out in the desert, lost, or lying suffocated in the sand.

'Can we really say why we do a certain thing, or follow the lure of a whisper in the night? The only safety, Lady Wilde, would be to stay in a chair, in a room, with all the doors locked and all the windows barred. Then we might escape life and never have to meet with danger ... but life and danger are the meat and drink of our very souls, and this makes us the most primitive hunters on earth, following a scent only our senses are aware of, obeying an impulse as undeniable as the earth demanding rain. If this were not so, then why did you come again to Persia?'

Grace stared at him. 'How did you know – how could you know I had been to Persia before? We had never met before my husband hired you to superintend our trip into the desert.'

'Quite so,' he said. 'We never met in the sense that we were introduced, but our paths crossed, when you were not the titled lady of an English lord.'

Grace stared at him ... surely his was a face that once seen was not easily forgotten! Those eyes, that beard, the rather arrogant way he carried himself ... she would surely not have forgotten him had she seen him during her tour of Persia three years ago, when she had been a carefree girl of nineteen and unaware, even, of Tony's existence.

'I have no recollection of you beyond that day at Reza Shahr, when my husband hired you.' She spoke coldly, for something in his manner was beginning to have a most disturbing effect upon her. In the most subtle way imaginable he was letting her know that she was a woman alone and very much in his hands. All about them the desert brooded like an animal that had slaked its hunger and was now sprawled with its claws in the sand, ready to slumber, or to lash out again. The atmosphere held menace indescribable, and Grace could feel a cry for Tony welling up inside her. Though he didn't love her, he was familiar to her, and his drawling English voice could never make strange sensations creep up and down her spine as did the deep, gravelly voice of this tall Persian.

'Oh, what's going to happen?' she gasped. 'How long is it since your men went searching for my husband? It seems hours!'

'For those who wait it always seems like hours,' he said. 'Rustam could make coffee if we were fortunate enough to be within sight of some camelthorn bushes, or other means of making a fire. But as you can see this part of the desert is quite desolate and we must wait, if we wait all night, for my men to return. Fold my cloak and sit upon it. Try to be as comfortable and relaxed as possible, Lady Wilde. You will only burn up energy if you pace about and think only of the worst.'

'I – I couldn't possibly rest.' Her eyes appealed to him for some sort of understanding, but his face was still a bronze mask, revealing no hint of pity for her or Tony. He was inhuman, made of stone instead of flesh and feeling!

'You keep your human emotions under mortice lock,' she flared. 'And I don't doubt that the key was thrown away years ago!'

'Be angry if it helps.' His voice was as unemotional as his face. 'Tears I have always regarded as an idle indulgence, but anger, fury, these are active emotions.'

'Yes, in tune with your desert ways,' she stormed at him, a wave of truant hair falling into her eyes, and her hands thrust into the pockets of her breeches so his keen eyes wouldn't see that they were trembling. Her entire body felt at the mercy of her racked nerves, and because this man Kharim was as hard as iron she didn't mind letting loose her temper on him ... her Tillerton temper inherited from

63

Jonas, who had never pretended to be a gentleman but who had wanted his granddaughter to be a lady. Right now Grace didn't feel ladylike. She felt a hatred of the desert and of the men who were part of its cruelty.

'The desert can be brutal.' Kharim took a leather case from a pocket in his robe and selected from it a dark-leaved cheroot. He struck a match and lit the cheroot, which emitted a smoke with an almost lethal tang to it. 'So can it be wondered at, milady, that men born of the desert are tough, fatalistic, often merciless? We all, in one way or another, exhibit the temperament of our birthplace.'

'And I take it you were born in the desert,' she said. 'Somehow I couldn't imagine you being born anywhere else.'

'True, I was born in the very heart of it, and the first thing I saw when my eyes were fully open was a desert star. I would say that it has led me ever since on a quest for – heaven.'

To hear such words from the hard lips of this man, in a voice that seemed to rake its way over her very skin, was almost shocking to Grace. Shocking because unexpected. Shocking because a few hours ago he had taken orders from her . . . and now he was giving them, and saying the sort of things no man had ever said to her.

She brushed at the golden disorder of her hair, and the gold ring gleamed on her hand in the sultry light of the sun as it came out from behind the sand-clouds, sulky and red-tinged. It was probably a touch of hysteria, but Grace had an overwhelming, mid-Victorian impulse to remind this man that she was a married woman and she expected to be treated as such. She wasn't to be taken advantage of because her husband was missing. She came of an influential family and wasn't any little nobody who had wandered into the desert. Oh lord! She caught her bottom lip between her teeth. Here she was thinking along the same lines as Mrs. Landon St. John and her dire warnings at the Ambassador's ball. Grace had gulped back a laugh at the time and had thought it highly absurd that her projected trip should be

64

viewed as an invitation to abduction.

'Men are men,' Mrs. Landon St. John had said in her loud and knowing voice. 'More so in certain places than in others, so be a sensible girl and forget this nonsense about seeing "the real desert". It could be more dangerous than you realize, and you're not exactly equipped for that kind of danger.'

'What do you mean by "that kind of danger"?' Grace had had to make an effort to keep her face in order, for there under the bright chandelier with the music playing, she knew full well what Mrs. Landon St. John was implying, and the whole conception seemed as absurd as a silent movie serial.

'You're a romantic!' The travelled and cynical old lady had snapped out the word as if it were an expletive. 'You're at the mercy of your emotions, and your good looks, if you did but know it, and you harbour the absurd notion that happiness can be sought in the desert of all places! Happiness is in yourself or it's nowhere, and I'd advise you, my girl, to settle for what you have — a title you can flaunt and money in your pocketbook. They'll always be your pass-key into the best houses, the most famous fashion salons, and the better restaurants, for as you grow older you'll learn that romance is another word for heartache, and that love bears the same initial as loneliness. There's no finding either of those in the dusty desert — there's no lost garden of Sheba and Solomon, for if there were some bright lad would have turned it into a tourist attraction by now and made his fortune.'

The cynicism of the words stung Grace as she remembered them . . . she had gone searching for a little happiness, but in its stead she had found torment and a terrible anxiety . . . and something else from which her mind and her entire nervous system shrank. It stood there in the shape of a man . . . and only a few hours ago Grace would have scorned the very notion that she could ever feel a chill uncertainty of a man's intentions.

Now, for the second time in her life, she felt as uncertain

as if she stood at the edge of a high precipice and was being dared by fate to leap off. The last time she had felt this sense of a void at her feet had been the day of her marriage to Tony. She had known that she was taking a step she would be bound to regret, and once again at the oasis she had taken a false step . . . and there was no turning back! She stood at bay between the relentless and unknown desert . . . and a man who belonged to that desert as the very sands did, as the thrusting, powerful palm trees did, as the ardent heat by day and the long cool winds of night, following the opulent sunsets through the darkness to the breathless dawn.

Grace stared at the desert, for now she was gripped by a terror of facing this man named Kharim . . . this man who was not a guide . . . who knew that last night she had fought with her husband. Her limbs felt as if they were yielding to a sort of quicksands, and her eyes felt as if they were seeing ghosts, riding in over the hot, hazy sands on horses so swift they appeared to fly.

As the quicksands gripped her and seemed as if they would pull her down to her knees, hands caught at her, held her, saved her from falling, for as the horsemen came nearer she saw the inert figure strapped across the haunches of the central horse, with its rider crouched forward in the saddle.

She knew, as the gripping hands knew, that the terrible desert had claimed her husband, and Kharim's men were returning with his lean, elegant, lifeless body.

# CHAPTER FIVE

THEY had entered a gorge that rose stark on either side of
the caravan, a dry and gloomy tunnel of rock along which
echoed every jingle of the harness, every scrape of a hoof on
stone, every murmur and mutter of a male voice.

Along this narrow trail, with sheer cliff dropping into
infinity at the side of it, they went on foot with the animals
strung out behind them. Grace had known for hours that
they weren't heading in the direction of Reza Shahr, but she
spoke no word, uttered no complaint, and bore the hardship
of the trek as if it were only to be expected that she should
be punished. Her head felt heavy and yet light, and every
single nerve in her body was like a strung wire, humming
with tension.

In the wildest of dreams she could not have imagined
such a nightmare end to her trip . . . Tony lay forever buried
where the sandstorm had struck them; buried deep so the
jackals wouldn't get at his body, his restless desires and his
greeds quiet at last, as his face had been strangely quiet, the
eyes closed tight from the pressure of the sand which had
suffocated him, the light of his mocking and careless soul
snuffed out like a candle in the wind.

Kharim had then given orders that they proceed to a
water-hole, where they had camped in the sunset and spent
the night. Now it was daylight again, and they were trekking
away from the civilization of the town where friends would
have offered sympathy and comfort; they were heading into
the heart of the desert, and Grace had neither the heart nor
the will to protest. All she felt was an unbearable guilt . . . it
was as if she had unloaded her tiny revolver in Tony's face
and struck the love of living from his eyes.

The path ahead twisted and turned like a maze, and the
cliffs were so towering they almost shut out the blaze of the
sun far overhead. Grace's gaze travelled all the way up to

the sky, so that when the path turned she stumbled and almost fell against the man who walked ahead of her.

'Oh!' She reached out a hand to save herself, and felt it firmly clasped, holding her from the edge of the gorge.

'What are you trying to do?' The voice was harsh. 'You would indeed break your neck if you fell down there!'

The lash of his words combined with the sheer misery which she felt brought a rush of tears to her eyes, too quickly for her to be able to blink them away. Kharim saw them glistening in her eyes, and his arm seemed to clench about her body ... not in concern for her, she learned a second later, but in concern for the trek.

'You have pain from a twisted ankle?' he demanded. 'There are fallen rocks on this path and you stumbled—'

'Against you, that's all.' His curt tone of voice dried away her tears before they could make a weeping fool of her. 'You can let go of me – please, take your arm away!'

He studied her face, which was totally without colour; a small mask, still stamped with the shock of the moment when they had lifted Tony from the horse to which they had strapped him and she had seen the total stillness of his features, closed against life for ever more ... a man not her lover, but a man to whom she had been married.

'Don't act the martyr if you have hurt yourself – any small *maladie* in the desert can soon develop into a disablement, and I think you had better remove your boot so I can examine your ankle.'

'My ankle is perfectly fine,' she protested. 'Are you now a medicine man as well as a guide?'

'I am a qualified vet, milady, and you would be surprised how much a highly strung filly and a woman have in common. They both have emotional natures and fine-boned ankles – now, you will stamp that foot so I may be assured that you are able to walk without limping, until we are out of the gorge and able to ride again. Come, I am sure a good stamp will help to release some of that bottled-up hatred you feel for me.'

Looking right at him, and with vigour, Grace stamped

her left foot, then her right one. Some of the proud spirit welled into life again, and now her eyes came alive with temper instead of tears. 'And where do you think you're taking me? I'm not such a fool that I take this for the tourist route back to Reza Shahr.'

'You came into the desert to seek escape from the sort of people at Reza Shahr,' he said deliberately. 'Return among them and once again you will find yourself involved with a man who makes promises and always breaks them. Society is like that, it has turned truth into the easily spoken lie, and made the lie an excuse never to be responsible for the truth. Here in the desert there are no pretensions; a man is a man, and a woman is a woman. There is only the sky lit by the stars instead of neons; only the sands, soft as down when the temper of the desert is soft, cruel if the desert wills it so. The desert is the garden of Sheba, and you hired a man, did you not, to show you the garden where Sheba was loved by Solomon?'

'But that – that was before my husband—' Grace stared at the bronze hauteur of Kharim's face, the force of the features strangely at odds with the eyes that should have been as dark as the rest of him. Their jade clarity, their depth and yet their density, filled Grace with a strange fear of him. Who are you? she wanted to cry out. Who the *devil* are you?

'I now hate the desert—' She gave a visible shudder. 'It killed my husband, and all I feel is a sense of – threat. I don't wish to go further into the desert. I wish to leave it, so you will order the men to turn about and take the route to Reza Shahr!'

'My orders are already given, Lady Wilde.' A gleam of mocking amusement flickered in his eyes, a little like lightning playing over the surface of deep water. 'Do you think I'd change them at the command of a mere woman? You never hired me, for I was never to be hired. I chose to take charge of the expedition planned by your husband, and now that Lord Wilde is dead, I am in charge of you. This is the desert, milady. Here the rules are different, and the laws.

Those laws are as old as Adam and we continue to abide by them, especially in the case of a woman.'

As he paused, as if to let his words sink into her mind, her nerves, her very senses, she tautened as if like an arrow drawn on a bowstring. From her booted feet, upwards to the very roots of her hair, she was poised as if for flight.

'What are you talking about?' she demanded. 'I don't understand you!'

'On the contrary, I think you understand me very well. When a woman loses her husband in the desert, the head of a caravan then becomes responsible for her. He provides shelter for her and sees that she wants for nothing. He assumes almost the right of another husband.'

'You – you can't be serious?' That sense of nightmare rushed over Grace again ... everything, every ache and every fear, was terribly real, and yet they had to be unreal, part of a fevered dream from which she must awake. She swayed, and the arm that was like iron was locked around her again, holding her from the rim of the gorge, holding her from that deep fall that comes in sleep and wakes the sleeper from the nightmare.

'Let me go ... let me go!' She struggled with him, and with an abrupt oath he swung her from her feet, and the next moment she lay over his shoulder and he was striding along the narrow path, holding her to him with an arm across the back of her thighs ... like a bundle of blankets.

'You damn brute!' she sobbed. 'You'll be thrown in jail when the authorities hear of this – this outrage!'

'There has been no outrage – yet,' he replied. 'Consider yourself fortunate that you are in my hands and not those of one of the unscrupulous fellows who do prey upon tourists. At least I wash my hands and keep the grime out of my fingernails.'

The strength of his hands, and the length of his stride, were enough in themselves to add fear to indignity ... but his words held a sort of grim humour, as of a man who knew entirely the risks involved in carrying off a woman who was not of the desert and not to be treated as if desert laws applied to her.

'You'll love it in jail,' she choked. 'Four walls all around you and no desert sky above you. I shouldn't think any woman was worth that, least of all one who hates the sight of you. Are you so hard up for a woman that you have to resort to kidnap? It's a terrible crime and you'll be locked up for years!'

'I wish you would lock up your lips – or shall I do it for you?' he asked. 'We don't rub noses in the Persian desert, you know. Be quiet, girl, and accept what was predicted even before you left Reza Shahr. Who will be surprised . . . who will really care? Already the young Captain will have found a new diversion, and the old lady with the loud voice will have become immersed in new gossip. Already it will be known at Reza Shahr that a bad sandstorm hit the desert . . . it will come as no surprise if the caravan of Lord and Lady Wilde were lost and never seen again, for let me assure you that more than one Englishwoman has disappeared into the desert never to be heard of again.'

'Is that your plan for me?' she demanded breathlessly. 'that I am to – to disappear into the desert – with you?'

'Yes – does the plan not appeal to you?' He spoke as casually as a man about town offering a girl a spin in his sports car. It was all so incredible that Grace had to stop thinking about it, or go out of her mind. She closed her eyes and felt the jogging motion as she was carried along like something this barbarian had captured . . . as in the far-off days of Tamara and Darius, not to mention Ahmed the Golden! An hysterical desire to laugh or scream welled up in Grace . . . choked off as she was set upon her feet to find they had emerged from the gorge into the sudden brilliant sunlight of the open desert. There it lay ahead of them, flaming red sandstone and rolling hillocks of golden sand, lit from above by the pure azure of the sky, swept clean of yesterday's sultry clouds, like the brow of a ruthless seductress.

As they stood there, with the open desert stretched at their feet, a wild hawk cried in the sky, and Grace could feel

71

the cry echoing through her body. And yet at the same time she was spellbound by the immense, undulating waves of tawny sand, cloth-of-gold across which they would ride, leaving embroidered in it the hoof marks of their mounts, and the heart-shaped pads of the camels.

Where did it lead to, this golden desert that lay beyond the shadowy gorge?

Her eyes found the face of Kharim, and with the desert light full upon him, caught in his eyes, in the sculptured folds of his robe and glinting in the ropes that bound his head-covering, he had the air of a Saadian prince as he surveyed the desert of blood-red rock and lion-pelted sand. He had about him the stillness and the golden savagery of it all . . . to this he belonged . . . to this he had brought her.

His eyes swooped, like those of that wild hawk overhead, and held her so she couldn't move. 'Whatever happens is written in the sand, and then the wind blows and the words change. Words of love or hate . . . words of grief or joy . . . from moment to moment. Life is forever restless, like that bird up there. Cruel and unpredictable. We of the desert accept this, and you, my Lady Wilde, will have to learn to do so.'

'What,' she asked tensely, 'would have happened if my husband had not been killed? Did you plan to take a hand yourself, if the sandstorm had not done the work for you?'

'The pattern of my plan was a loosely knit one,' he said drily. 'It was no secret at Reza Shahr that Lord Wilde had made plans of his own, and I would merely have forestalled him and he would have been the one to be lost . . . for a while, that is, until one of my men conveniently found him and escorted him back to Reza Shahr . . . minus his lady.'

'So all along—?'

'Yes, all along,' he agreed, with not a change of expression.

'You – you're unutterably brazen about it,' she said, in a low shaken voice that seemed disembodied from the crying protest inside her. 'Why pick on me – why?'

'Come now,' he mocked, his eyes raking over her slim

figure in the white silk shirt and the finely tailored fawn breeches, ending in the wine-coloured knee-boots. His eyes flicked upwards again to her pale heart of a face, the fair hair tucked beneath a brimmed hat. 'Don't pretend to me that a society lady has the modesty of a country maid. You know well enough that you're a beauty. The very clothes you wear are a foil for that slender frame, that white and flawless skin, and the hair that when unfurled shimmers around your face and neck like desert gold itself. Last, but certainly not least, there are your eyes. In a land of dark eyes, your blue gaze is like the promise of a pool in the heart of the burning sands; a mirage of cool bliss, a caress of limpid heaven, a dip into seas so deep there is no finality. My lady, when your spoiled and foolish boy of a husband let it be known that he was seeking horses for a journey into the desert, I would have been less than a son of the desert if I had not held out my hand for the lustrous golden plum that Allah dropped into it.

'A guide?' He threw back his head and his laughter held the cruel mockery and scorn of Darius himself. 'I am Kharim Khan, and paramount chief of my tribe, the Haklyt Rohim. In this the Land of the Peacock Throne and the King of Kings, I am more powerful than even you may imagine. For me the abduction of a mere girl is a *bagatelle*. I could be assassinated at any time, having enemies who hate me as you could never dream of hating anyone, even such as me, a man of a desert nation who saw you – and wanted you!'

With these words he clicked his fingers and one of his men swiftly brought their mounts. 'Now we ride,' he said, and when he took a step towards Grace, she turned at once to her mount, found the stirrup and swung into the saddle. Argument with such a man was useless . . . she must in due course find some other way to elude him. Her fingers gripped the reins, a tingling sensation in them, for she was seeing far more of the Orient than she had dreamed of. Its ruthless climate had already laid its lash across her back, and now she found herself the unwilling, afraid but defiant

73

captive of a *khan*, as ruthless as the desert which had bred him; as subtle and as unpredictable. She didn't doubt that at last he had told the truth about himself . . . as he mounted he had the look of a centaur; brown, strong arms emerging from a tunic with divided sleeves, and on the forefinger of his right hand he wore a sombre-stoned seal ring which caught the sun as he raised his arm in a signal that the caravan proceed. Deep in that stone glowed the redness of blood and fire and danger.

Deep in the man glowed the realities that a gem could only reflect . . . a shiver, an instant of fearful self-doubt ran through Grace. Could she possibly find some way to escape those strong and daring hands that had reached out across the sands and caught her in their hold as a heartless boy might trap a fish or a butterfly?

They rode forward into the still, hot air of the afternoon, and for the present Grace was resolved to concentrate on the desert and to try and ignore the various fears that were knocking at her heart. She saw growing in stony beds bushes so crimson they seemed to be on fire in the sun. And for contrast the sudden steely glitter of a water-course, or a patch of pure lemon-coloured sand, thrown like a strand of pale silk against the rough, spread lion-skin of the surrounding desert. Far off were mountains, thrusting dark-blue turrets into the sky, like immense castles empty of humanity.

If that was the Mountain of Mercy, thought Grace, then it had a strange and unrelated name. It was dark and merciless as the profile of Kharim Khan; aloof in the burning sunlight, with an attraction almost terrible, so that the eyes were forced to look and wonder.

'We say of this – *khàsh-gol*.' The words were flung suddenly over the broad shoulder. 'Good earth, harsh and yet beautiful. Or do you disagree, Lady Wilde?'

'It has a terrible beauty,' she agreed. 'Savage and tawny, like a great cat with an uncertain temper.'

The *khan* glanced round at her and his eyes had narrowed against the dark-tawny skin of his face. He knew that she referred to him and not to the desert, and his eyes glinted with the green devilry of a large feline, sure of itself and its prey.

'You are not without a temper yourself — I have both heard it, and seen it flash in your eyes, like summer lightning. With your temperament you must make friends with the desert. It won't do if you fight its fascination and restrain your impulse to be fascinated. The desert is a strange place, a sphinx who knows its friends and its enemies.'

'You mean,' she said coldly, 'that the desert takes care of its own, and you are assuredly one of those, aren't you? But I am not! I'm English, and you can't force me to like your cruel and relentless desert, no more than you can enforce me to like you. Is that what you're hoping for, Kharim Khan? That I shall become as afraid of you, and as quick to obey you as your people?'

'Hope is like the desert flower, milady.' He reined his stallion so that Grace's mount drew abreast with him. 'It shoots up swiftly when conditions permit, blooms for only a short space of time, and then shrivels away to dust. We of the desert don't live on hope.'

'So you're implying that you can make me obedient to your laws.' Grace gave the scornful toss of the head which had always put Tony in a fury, but this man merely flicked her face with his eyes, as a hand might flick a bothersome fly, and a slight smile curled on his lips and then was gone.

'Having made men obedient to my laws, as you call them, I see no difficulty in making a mere girl a trifle more amenable to my ways.'

'You'll be lucky,' she flung at him. 'You'll have to kill me, as the desert killed Tony, before I'll bend the knee to you. You? You're nothing but a barbarian! Someone who makes his own laws and lives only to suit his own whims. Well, I am English, and when *our* law catches up with you—'

'Do you really think it will?' He gestured lazily with his whip, indicating the desert that surrounded them on all sides, rolling plains of sand with outcrops of rock so red they

75

had the look of sacrificial stones, as if victims had shed their life blood upon them. In her frightened heart Grace knew that she could be taken deep into the desert, among a tribe of people so loyal to their *khan* that no murmur of her presence among them would ever leak to the outside world. She could literally disappear, and be presumed lost and dead by her grandfather, by her friends, and by those at Reza Shahr who had warned her not to travel with a husband who was not to be trusted.

While everyone had been busy warning her against Tony, the 'guide' in charge of the trek had been weaving his own subtle web of deception . . . and now she must weave her own in order to escape him. She thought of the small, pearl-handled revolver in her luggage . . . the night before last she would have found the nerve to shoot Tony through the shoulder had he touched her with hands that shook from all that cognac . . . the hands that held the reins of the big dappled grey were brown and firm, and Grace fiercely told herself that they would never touch her skin. They would never travel dark and long-fingered over her body . . . as soon as he gave the order for camp to be struck, she would ask for her pigskin case and arm herself with the little gun. Thank the lord she knew how to use it. Jonas had been ruthlessly practical about that, and she knew the vulnerable places of the human body . . . the position of the heart that beat beneath the sun-browned skin of Kharim Khan was no mystery to her, and she would aim for his heart and empty his green eyes of mockery and male assurance. She would topple his tall, proud body to the sands, and his last murmur, his last caress, would be for the tawny skin of his savage desert.

'You smile, milady.' His voice cut like a whip across her thoughts. 'You have a mental picture of the gallant Captain Thorpe coming to your rescue, eh? Galahad in khaki riding his military camel. It is quite a picture, I agree. It makes me smile.'

'You – you mock everything,' she accused, and her eyes were storm blue beneath the brim of her hat, and gone was

76

all that earlier sense of enervation and deadly nausea, produced by images of Tony, mummified by the sand. She was the granddaughter of Jonas Tillerton, and therefore a fighter. She wouldn't depend on any man to execute her rescue . . . she would do that herself, or go down fighting.

'I mock not quite everything,' he denied. 'I dislike certain pretensions; the upper layers of brittle icing on the warm depths of life. I am contemptuous of the easy lie in place of the hard truth. The shrill, demanding voice of the so-called liberated woman in place of the deep warm tones of the sensuous 'slave' who walks in freedom as no city woman ever walked in her narrow, high heels. I dislike your world, Lady Wilde, as much as you dislike mine – at present. A dislike, I venture to add, which is centred in me rather than in the desert. You would not have returned to Persia had you not felt a desire to do so.'

'I wish to heaven I had never returned! I – it was my idea, and now my husband is dead and I'm to blame. Perhaps,' Grace shrugged her shoulders, 'it's just as well I don't have to face friends just yet. They might be too kind, but there's no danger of that from you, is there?'

Instead of replying to her question he looked at her with a raised eyebrow. 'There are several kinds of danger I might offer, yet you fear my kindness. Strange that anyone so lovely should have met with so little kindness from men. It is a state of affairs to be remedied – in due course.'

Each word he spoke seemed to play on her nerves; each glance he gave her was a subtle threat and a promise. What was his idea of kindness? Surely not a shoulder for a woman to rest upon, so that for once in her life she might know the total security of someone she could trust! This man was more treacherous than anyone she had ever known! He had assumed a mask to deceive her, and that was something neither Jonas nor Tony had ever done. They had been honest with her, even if they had never loved her.

'I'd no more trust your kindness than the outstretched paw of a leopard,' she said scornfully. 'Stay in character, Kharim Khan. I prefer the real face to the mask of Judas.'

'Do you know, milady, that if my men understood your English words, they would expect me to punish you.' He spoke with a dry, yet menacing edge to his voice.

'With the whip?' she asked airily. 'I had heard of your sort of desert tyrant on my first visit to Persia; men who fear and dislike the advance of progress because it will inevitably put an end to their own despotic way of life. It seemed incredible to me, then, that in these modern times people could still live entirely bound by the desert, under the sway of a single man, but I see now that I was wrong to be sceptical. The desert is still spacious enough, and untamed enough to hold a tyrant, isn't it?'

'Exactly so.' He spoke curtly, but he was no longer looking at her, for his attention had been caught by the two men who had been riding ahead of the caravan, and who had now halted and were sitting still in the saddle, bronze images in their fawn robes, outlined against the sky that was turning opalescent as the sun began to cool for its daily dying. They waited upon a high sandy ridge edged with shrubs of thorn, and below them there seemed to be a valley. Grace felt a strange quickening of her pulse, for with a bound Kharim Khan's horse had obeyed the light slap of his hand and a moment later he was beside his men, and his eyes were surveying what lay below that ridge.

It seemed to Grace as she rode towards him that he had an air of magnetic authority; it seemed to electrify everyone, for the jingling of harness became louder as hands tightened on the reins of horse and camel, and the voices of the men rose out of their throats, the occasional mutter of words giving way to an eager wave of talk.

'Come!' the *khan* called out to Grace. 'And as you come, close your eyes and don't give me an argument!'

'What nonsense—' Yet she obeyed him, and her mount climbed the ridge with the nervous eagerness of a dry horse scenting water and oats. Her own senses were curiously avid and aroused in that moment, and then she felt a hand grasping her reins.

'Now you may look, milady, and never dare to say to my

face again that I am my people's tyrant.'

Grace opened her eyes and there below them, stretched out in an immense golden bowl, were an incredible number of long black tents. Seen from above their erection was a miracle of exactitude, line upon line of them, the dwellings of goat-hair in which each family ate and slept and spent their lives when they were not on the move with their huge flocks of sheep, and goats.

'The Haklyt Rohim,' said the man at Grace's side. 'A tribe as old as Adam, with a pride and strength, a courage and independence which could only be dissipated in the modern cities of so-called progress. You call it that, when it is really a searching after false idols to worship. Here in the desert the Haklyt Rohim have the wild free air to breathe, the food provided by their animals, the joy of their families, and their ancient songs and stories. My men have the very best horses to ride, and now and again the excitement of a skirmish with the soldiery, or with rogues who would plunder the livestock. We have no night clubs here, Lady Wilde. No bars or casinos, but we manage, believe it or not, to be strangely in love with our way of life.'

He paused, his hand still firm upon the reins of her mount, holding him back from the rim of the ridge. 'Were you ever in love with yours?' he asked deliberately.

'Whatever my life,' she said tensely, 'you had no right – no right in the world to drag me away from it. Whatever your methods with your own women, they become a crime when applied to me – and you know it! I'm not some *harem* slave who comes willingly to your tent, Kharim Khan, seduced by the image of silk cushions and the scent of sandalwood. I didn't come into the desert for *that*!'

'I wonder if you do truly know what you came for.' His tone of voice was sardonic, and with an abrupt movement of his right hand he gave the order for the caravan to move down the hill to the vast encampment of his people. With his hand still upon her reins he led Grace's mount on the heels of his own. Her eyes hated him in his deep blue robes, his headcloth bound with ropes in which there must have been

79

strands of gold, for they caught the setting rays of the sun and glistened, as the huge seal ring glistened on his hand.

As they came within scent and sound of the tents, women and children came out, and men came hurrying from the direction of the herds. The smoke of the coffee fires lay over the camp like a veil, musky with dried juniper wood, aromatic with the flavour of the spices in the coffee pots. Children ran to touch Kharim's boots, and the women smiled with a shyness of gazelles in the presence of a magnificent buck. The men flung greetings in their deep, staccato voices, and there rushed over Grace the awareness that nothing the man did would ever be condemned by these dark-eyed, brown, supple and untamed people who lived as their forebears of a thousand suns ago had lived. Close to the earth, to the elements, to the vital beating heart of all the passions.

Grace could feel their dark eyes upon her, and suddenly, so that she flinched, Kharim Khan whipped the hat from her head, and the last red rays of the sun merged with the fairness of her hair as it tumbled around the pallor of her face and neck.

*She will come riding fair on a horse of fire, and the people will know her for the bride of the dark one.*

As these words flashed through Grace's brain, her mount was brought to a halt in front of a large tent that stood separate from the rest. It was of goat-hair like the rest, but dyed a brilliant turquoise blue, and its entrance and its exit were covered by striped silk hangings.

Kharim Khan swung long legs to the ground and before Grace had recovered from the surprise of the huge blue tent, he was beside her chestnut horse and holding out an imperative hand for her to grasp.

'I – I can manage without your assistance,' she defied him. 'Get out of my way!'

'Don't speak to me like that, and don't be a child. I know you are stiff from those long hours in the saddle and if you attempt to dismount without my assistance you will surely stumble and fall on your face. Is that how milady wishes to be seen by the Haklyt Rohim, stretched on her face at my feet?'

'You – you're the devil himself!' Grace accused, and his touch was more unbearable than anything had been as she allowed him to assist her to the ground. She was stiff, and weary in every limb, aching all over for a long hot bath, and parched for a long cool drink. It swept over her that right now she was helpless in his hands; she had to submit to his immediate dictates and try to outwit him when she had regained her strength and courage.

The smouldering sun was dropping behind the distant peaks, and shadows were creeping over the desert. Soon the sky would be as black as onyx, and soon she would be alone with Kharim Khan.

A shiver ran all through her, and his keen eyes didn't miss the quivering of her face and her body. 'We are camped in the Dasht-i-Sheb, which we call the desert of Sheba, and though the sun is so hot by day, a wind begins to blow at night. You don't want to take a chill, so come into the blue tent and be welcome.'

'No—' She backed away from him, and she could feel the terror waking in her again. 'Can't I stay elsewhere – in another tent? You can't seriously mean to – to keep me with you? It would be unendurable! I won't stand for it!'

'You will fall if you don't enter my tent and rest yourself. You will walk, milady, or I shall carry you inside. Which do you prefer?'

A single glance at the adamant set of his features was enough to convince her that he meant what he said. Grace gave a wild look around her . . . she had never condoned fox-hunting, and right now she felt rather like a trapped fox. Dark eyes were fixed upon her, curious, intrigued, alien, and possibly unaware that she was a victim of the *khan's* audacity rather than his willing guest.

'You shame me!' she gasped.

'It hasn't yet come to that,' he drawled, and holding aside a flap of the tent he indicated that the moment had come for her to walk inside or be carried. Hating him with her eyes, with every nerve in her slim body, she walked into the big blue tent and felt the toes of her boots sink into the lush rugs covering the floor. Above her head hung oil-lamps, flames bright as gold in the globes of them, playing their light over the fitments of a chief's tent.

With a toss of her head she wanted to feel contemptuous of it all, but she had been taught too well to recognize beauty, and it lay in the pheasant-tail brilliance of Tabriz hangings and Shiraz carpets. In the antique miniatures grouped on a mother-of-pearl inlaid table. In the glow of a blue Persian vase, and the exquisitely carved set of chessmen on a low table beside a long divan, across which was flung a scarlet saddlecloth.

Her nostrils tensed to an aroma of spice, leather, cheroot smoke and lamp oil. Each scent was part of the carpets, the hangings, the big cushions scattered on the divan. The tent had an air of being lived in, and Grace could feel the clenching of her hands, the stab of her fingernails in her palms as she visualized a long, lean, supple male body sprawled on the divan, the smoke of a cheroot climbing about the hard, sculptured features and losing itself in the tapestry that hung behind the divan, whose silky surface featured lovers reclining beneath pomegranate trees, and strolling hand in hand beside lotus pools. It hung there in a kind of sensuous glory, worked by the slender hands of a lady of the harem, as beautiful and antique as the rest of the things that Kharim Khan liked to have about him, even here in the desert, so that he might relax in the glow of them after a long day in the saddle.

She heard a movement behind her as the tent flap fell into place, and she swung round and all awareness of the fitments of the blue tent were lost in the overwhelming effect which the *khan* had, standing tall against the closed entrance to his dwelling, his wide shoulders barring the way out.

Grace thought of herself slung across his shoulder like a doe he had caught while out hunting, and she wanted to scream, yell, call him every bad name she could think of. As the Tillerton temper flared alight in her veins, so did the awareness that he expected her to give way to an emotional

82

storm. She saw the deep gleam of diablerie in his green eyes, and at once her lips compressed and she forced back the stormy words and strove to be ice-cool and stony as a statue. He would like that less than a hot flare of temper. He was of the desert and he understood passion far more than the coldness of pure hatred.

'Now what?' She stood there as cold and straight as on the day she had stood beside Tony Wilde and heard the priest declare that she now belonged to a man for whom she felt not a spark of love. 'Am I to be ravished on the divan?'

'Is that what you'd like?' he asked mockingly. 'And please don't throw that vase near your hand – it's priceless.'

'I wouldn't cheapen myself by throwing things, like a fishwife,' she said, with cold scorn. 'But I don't imagine you brought me here to play chess with you – I see from that *maille* over there that your tent has its *harem* section!'

His eyes followed the contemptuous flick of her hand to the curtain of long blue beads that divided the tent. Finely strung to form a mesh that could not be seen through . . . a web for a pretty fly.

'Did you hope that you would be my first female guest?' he mocked. He moved then, with that animal grace of a big man at the peak of fitness, throwing off his cloak and letting it fall into a careless blue heap to the floor. He stood revealed then in his tunic and breeches, and he ducked his tall covered head to avoid the hanging lamps as he trod the deep-pile carpets in Grace's direction. Grace couldn't help but notice the animal grace with which he moved, and this, perversely, was one more mark against him. A man in his position, with the outward trappings of distinction and leadership, should have more control over his personal caprices.

Grace had never known the indignity before of being a mere caprice, and her icy coldness was swamped by fury, and her eyes shone brilliant with temper against the pallor of her face. 'Did you hope that I'd feel flattered to be here?' she demanded. 'Did you suppose that I'd find it thrilling to be abducted and brought to your den in the desert? All I feel

83

is degradation and insult, and at the very first chance I'll—' She broke off on the very verge of saying she would put a bullet through him, for he mustn't know that she had a small gun in her luggage. If he knew he would soon take it away and she would be left entirely defenceless.

'At the very first chance you will do – what?' His eyes had narrowed in that almost terrifying way, glittering green like a leopard's eyes when it prepares to spring upon its prey.

'Run away,' she flung at him, with a toss of her hair, fair and unruly about her temples and her neck, making her fretfully aware of how untidy she must look, how hot and bothered, how far removed from the cool and gracious person she normally appeared. 'I'll run, Kharim Khan, and I shan't care if the desert kills me!'

'I should care,' he said drily. 'Each man they say has one inherent weakness, and mine is that I like beautiful things. Tactile things that I can take into my hands and admire.' His eyes swept her from head to toe, and it was a look that stripped the shirt and breeches from her body and saw the skin and delicate curves that no man had yet touched . . . not even the man who had been her husband.

Instinctively she backed away from that look and gave a little gasp as she was brought up short against the divan table. Her body jarred it and a couple of the chess pieces fell over . . . as they fell her nerves cried out for an end to this torment. Suddenly she wanted to plead with him to let her go . . . the pleading and the pride made war within her . . . her pride won, for her instincts told her that he was not a man to be moved by the pleas of a woman.

'I – we've been riding for hours.' She pushed at the hair that tumbled into her eyes. 'If only I might have a bath – if you have that much compassion? I – I can still feel the sand grains from yesterday, and today has been so hot.'

'Achmed, my personal servant, is already preparing water for your bath, milady.' Kharim Khan spoke lazily, with a touch of humour. 'I am fully aware that you like beyond anything to be clean and fresh, and if you will step into the other partition of my tent you will find there your suitcases, various requisites for a bath, and in a very short while a young woman will arrive to attend on you. I shall go myself to bath in the tent of my petty chief, Davoud Sayed. I too, Lady Wilde, have a fondness for a hot soak and a scrub, being not entirely the barbarian I have been called.'

With that subtle smile that could have meant anything, the *khan* touched long lean fingers to his eyes, his lips and his heart. '*Salaam alaykum*, milady. My house is yours — until I return.'

Those final words were almost whispered, and then he was gone, his long strides from the blue tent silenced by the thick rugs upon the floor. The flap fell into place behind his wide shoulders, and Grace was alone with the knowledge that he had left her for only a while. A strange, unsettled peace surrounded her in the tent, though beyond its walls she could hear the sound of voices and movement. The *khan* would have made sure that the tent was watched in case she tried to make a bolt for freedom. She smelled the smoke of the fires over which the food was cooking, and she felt within her the natural stirrings of hunger. For now she was powerless to get away, but as in the near distance she heard the soft clang of camel bells, a bronze music as the serpentine necks moved in the search for camelthorn, a thin thread of hope ran through her. She had learned to sit a camel, and she had the tiny gun. Tiny as it was, it could bring down a man . . .

# CHAPTER SIX

As Grace stood within the lamplit *harem* of the *khan*'s tent, she felt torn by a wild resentment at being here, and by a curiosity that would not be controlled by her contempt. Her eyes rested for fully a minute on the low, broad ottoman that was covered from head to foot by a dark fur throwover. Beside it stood a cedarwood chest, on which stood the lamps, a hammered silver box that probably contained those dark and lethal cheroots which he smoked, and a small beautiful copy of the Qur'an, with gold-edged pages and a gemmed clasp.

'Hypocrite!' Grace muttered, but her resentment of her host, her captor, could not be relieved even by the booted kick which she aimed at the carpet under her feet. Because it was glorious, and probably woven by a master, it seemed all the more hateful that it adorned the tent of Kharim Khan. There was a tree of life woven into the big rug, and this was rimmed by lovely Islamic symbols, such as peacocks and diamonds and the fabulous blue lotus. She wanted to hate it, and at the same time she wanted to sink down upon its thick, lush softness and give way to a storm of tears.

As the tears welled, as the impulse took possession of her, the bead curtain rattled and she spun round as sharply as if a snake had struck her shoulder.

A girl stood just within the curtain, and she was so darkly pretty that Grace's immediate reaction was that she 'belonged' to the *khan*; was his desert *kadin* who shared this room with him. She wore organza trousers and a short silk tunic, above which the blue *chaddur*, or veil, had been loosened to reveal her face. Her eyes were dark and lustrous, with a touch of kohl on the lids, and arching eyebrows like a pair of fine wings. Her skin was the colour of dark honey, and her black silky lashes made a fluttering movement as Grace studied her. She smiled shyly and her teeth were white and small against the dark red of her lips.

'My name is Shalena, and I am sent by the *agha* to assist the *lella* in her bathing.' The girl spoke in French, with a soft, lisping accent. 'If the *lella* will come into the little room of the bath she will find that everything is prepared and ready.'

As Grace stood there, still rebellious, still resentful of every member of the Haklyt Rohim, the girl moved with a soft chiming of ankle chains and shifted to one side a silk hanging in a corner of the room. At once Grace could smell the scented water, and as her entire body cried out for the relief and comfort of a hot bath, she set aside for the time being her nagging fears and sharp pricks of anger ... tormenting as the sand grains that she could feel against her skin.

Snatching up her pigskin dressing-case, she followed Shalena into the curtained alcove. There in the centre of it was her very own folding bath filled to almost the brim with scented, steaming water. On a low cane table stood jars and soaps and an immaculate loofah. Over a cane stool was draped a great, soft, fuzzy towel. In a corner stood a screen painted with blue and gold birds, and as Grace glanced at it, Shalena murmured that behind it was *la toilette*.

'Every home comfort,' Grace said cynically, and again when she looked at the Persian girl and caught a wisp of exotic, spicy perfume in her dark braided hair, the thought flitted across her mind that anyone as pretty as this would hardly escape the notice or the attention of the *khan*.

'Are you part of the household, Shalena?' she asked.

'*Oui, madame.*' Shalena smiled and fingered the gold and amber beads that hung around her neck, along with a chain on which hung a golden crescent set with a pearl.

'*Vous êtes très charmante,*' said Grace in her perfect French, to which she added in sarcastic English, 'Too much so to be a serving wench!'

'*Pardonnez-moi, madame?*' The girl looked faintly puzzled by the tone of Grace's voice. 'Is the *lella* angry about something? Is it that the bath water is too hot? She would

87

prefer it cold? The *agha* often has the water cold, so Achmed tells me, and I have heard that English people like this—'

'No, the water is fine.' Grace felt abruptly ashamed of herself for taking her temper out on this girl, who after all was subject to the *khan* and hardly in a position to be other than his obedient, even adoring slave. 'I wonder, Shalena, if I may have something cool to drink? My throat feels parched.'

'I am to bring whatever the *lella* desires. Perhaps a glass of the lemon sherbet which Achmed makes for my lord the *khan*? It is very refreshing.'

'Sounds ideal.' Grace broke into a smile, and listened to the music of the girl's anklets as she departed to fetch the drink. The bath stood waiting and without further hesitation Grace stripped off her dusty clothing and slipped into the fragrant, soothing water, which rose almost to her shoulders as she settled back for a good soak. The last time she had used this bath had been on the evening of her last quarrel with Tony. The memory was painful . . . her guilt was sharp . . . but still the most persistent feeling she had was the dread of Kharim Khan that lurked within her mind and her body. A tightening of nerves in the region of her midriff, a quickening of her heartbeats, a sense of that peculiar doom that only a woman can feel when she knows herself at the mercy of a man to whom women were merely objects of pleasure or service.

As her thoughts rose up to torment her, she splashed the bath water and gave herself a merciless scrubbing with the loofah and the translucent bar of palm-oil soap. It was as if she needed to scrub from her skin the touch of his hands when he had swung her over his shoulder, and when he had assisted her from her horse. She swore to herself that he wouldn't touch her again. Next time she would have the little gun on her person, and she fiercely told herself that she wouldn't care what his followers did to her so long as she evaded the *khan*'s arms . . . his dark, forceful closeness . . . the touch of his bearded lips on hers.

There was a swish of silk as Shalena returned, carrying a small tray of copper on which stood a glass in an attractive holder. 'Thank you,' said Grace. 'Put it on the table and I'll drink it when I've dried myself. You don't have to stay, Shalena. I can manage to dress myself.'

'But I have been told to wait on the *lella*,' the girl protested. 'It is my duty to do so.'

'Very well.' Seeing the flash of distress in the big brown eyes, Grace gestured at the adjoining room. 'You may open the big suitcase – the key is tied to it by a small piece of string – and lay out the dress I've decided to wear. It's dove-coloured, with a white collar and belt. There are dove-suede shoes in a bag to match, and stockings too.'

'What of jewellery, *madame*?'

'I shall not be wearing any.' Grace spoke firmly, and a trifle coldly. 'You must be aware, Shalena, that my husband died in the sandstorm, and that I am not here to – to decorate the tent of your *khan*. He said something about being responsible for me, that is all.'

'Yes, it is desert law, *madame*. You are now under the protection of the *khan*.' Shalena spoke as if this were a great honour, and Grace was glad when the girl slipped through the curtain into the bedchamber. That pretty, doe-eyed creature would be shocked and dismayed if Grace gave vent to her true feelings. If she cried out that she hated the very sight of the *khan*, and felt about as protected as a hare in a snare. The bath water made pools on the floor as she stepped out and swiftly draped herself in the huge towel. She then unbuttoned a little pocket in the breeches she had taken off before taking her bath, and took from the pocket a little key. This fitted the lock of her dressing-case, in which she carried those fateful pearls from Jonas, her gold-topped toiletries, her papers and passport in a slim leather case, her money, and the tiny gun with the pearl handle. There it lay, looking like a pretty toy, and yet as capable of killing a man as the sting of a venomous snake, or the angry lash of storm-driven sand.

As she caught the soft swish of silk, Grace swiftly closed

the case. But the sight of the gun made her feel more at ease, and with a slight smile she lifted the glass of lemon sherbet and started to drink it. It was delicious, with a real tang of lemons and a spicy dash of the East, and probably made from a recipe as old as the legend of Solomon and Sheba.

'I have brought Madame's underclothing.' Shalena stood holding the lacy slip and panties, as if waiting to assist Grace into them. 'The sherbet is good, *non*?'

'Exceedingly good.' Grace replaced the empty glass on the tray. 'You can run away now, Shalena. It won't take me five minutes to dress, and you can tell your master that you helped me.'

'May I not stay to help with the dressing of your hair, *madame*?'

'Are you so afraid of the man? Does he beat you if you dare to disobey his slightest whim?' Grace spoke with such cold scorn that Shalena backed away from her. Her eyes in their rim of kohl looked strangely perplexed for a moment, then she spun on her bare, hennaed heels and left Grace to manage on her own. Even as Grace gave a little sigh of relief at finding herself alone, she felt somewhat ashamed of herself for being so on edge. Her cool control seemed all but shattered, and she could feel the tremor in her limbs as she slipped into her undies, and then went through to the room where her evening dress was laid out. It shimmered a pool of soft grey on the dark fur coverlet of the low divan bed, and she snatched it up as if contact with the bed might contaminate the silk. She slid into it and quickly closed the tiny poppers at the waist. She settled the huge Quaker collar of snowy white so that it framed her throat and face, and made the belt snug about her waist in its real silver buckle.

The dress was a Pierre Cardin model purchased in Paris for her trip to Persia, and tonight it served a double purpose. There was a deep pocket concealed in the full silky skirt, and also the style and colour paid some tribute to Tony's death.

As she took her gold-backed hairbrush from her dressing-case, her hand clenched around it, taut with nerves, and cold as marble. She stared at the back of the brush, into which was beautifully incised a shining gold Eros, god of love, youth, divine sin. In a way Tony had been like that, in love with his own self, with his own sensations, and without any real sense of sin. He had been good-looking in his blond, sleek fashion, and her single consolation was that death had not ruined his appearance. His tomb of sand had stopped his breath before he could cry out, or his features be contorted by terror, and the *khan*'s men had buried him in astrakhan, for after all he had been a lord, with a title that stretched back down the years, and was now no more. There was no male relative to carry it on . . . no child of the marriage . . . for the marriage had been in name only.

Grace brushed her hair until the roots tingled, as if she had to inflict some measure of pain upon herself . . . like the widows of old who tore their hair. She wanted to feel the grief that came from a deep love, but in its place she felt guilt, and the awful regret of having been ruled by her pride. And pride came before a fall . . . and there was no denying that she had fallen into the hands of a devil far more dangerous and subtle than Tony had ever been.

A mirror stood on a cedarwood chest against a wall of the tent, and Grace stared at her reflection as if at the face of a stranger. Her hair like shining gilt was drawn back from the classic brow, the wide sweep of the fine dark brows above the deep blue eyes. The shapely nose was tensed to the many strange aromas above the full red lips. Cheekbones and jaw-line were firm yet feminine, as were the finely tapered collarbones.

Jonas had once said, with arrogant pride, that she had the cool beauty of the madonna lily . . . she might have been a lady born instead of the granddaughter of a back-street lad who from running errands for the gentry had gradually climbed over their backs to become bigger and richer than any of them.

Grace could look at herself with impersonal eyes because never had she been treated as a person by the man closest to her . . . Jonas Tillerton, toffee baron, ruler of a kingdom of tall smoking chimneys and factory shops filled with noisy machinery. Always for him Grace had been an object to improve upon .. as if like a candy she could be made sweeter, choicer, more decorative and lucrative. Her speech had to be that of the girls born to the high-class nobs of Manchester; her poise had to be even more natural than theirs; her knowledge had to be wider, and her heart had to be cooler. A warm heart, said Jonas, was more of a liability to a woman than an asset. It could rule her head, and turn it, and make her vulnerable in a society that preferred the diamond to the pearl; the smile to the tear; the satyr to the saint.

Now, thought Grace, the joke was on Jonas. Here in the desert there were no cool hearts and coronets; no ballrooms and chandeliers; no goose served up with champagne as she had been.

The goose, this time, stood ensnared in a harem tent, and her only defence was a tiny gun wrapped in a chiffon handkerchief in the pocket of a Quaker-girl dress. There were no pearls about her throat, no silver shoes upon her feet, no rose in her hair . . . as there had been the night of her introduction to Tony. Jonas had called her his fledgling turned into a swan . . . but even as she had walked down the curving staircase she had felt like a goose about to be gobbled up by a wolf.

That same feeling was upon her now, but intensified to a degree that was frightening. Because she was akin to Jonas Tillerton she had never really known what fear was . . . until she had been brought here to the desert tent of a man who was even more powerful, more ruthless and self-willed than Jonas himself. He awakened in Grace – to her angry shame – a sense of fear that went beyond the physical. It was a fear that touched the very nerves of her heart, so that each beat was like a low thunder in her breast; each small movement, as of a fly or a lizard on the blue walls of the tent, like a flick of lightning that made her flinch.

An hour or more had passed – her watch had stopped, possibly owing to the sand dust in the tiny, intricate works –

and she knew that soon the *khan* would return to his blue tent, to eat supper, to watch her with those startling green eyes in the face that was otherwise so dark, and to torment her until . . . until she was driven to use the little gun that lay beneath her hand in her pocket.

She stared at the thick *maille* of beads that separated the bedchamber from the main area of the tent, and then she looked around her again, and again that cold shiver ran through her body. 'Now don't be a craven, Grace.' She steeled her spine in the soft, silky armour of her grey dress, with the Quaker collar not much paler than the face which it framed.

For what was she searching? Grace wondered this as she took in once again the subtle splendour of this chamber in which the *khan* took his rest, and his pleasure. Was she hoping to find some evidence of another side to him? His French was that of an educated man, and he had said that he was a qualified veterinary surgeon . . . yet these civilized aspects seemed to mean nothing when set against this crime of abduction . . . this carrying off of an English woman to a desert valley, where the Haklyt Rohim were encamped in their thousands. He could hide her in such a place as easily as a needle in a bottle of sand, for not a single member of his tribe would breathe a word against him. In the desert a *khan* was as powerful as a king; so much Grace had learned on her previous visit to Persia. The *khans* had the deep loyalty of their people because very often they carried in their veins the same blood, and the same need for the freedom of the desert. Cities and towns meant nothing to them. They couldn't breathe in them, or ride through them on a spirited horse to their hearts' content. The city stars were blurred by smoke . . . dreams were choked to death by the civilized need to be possessed by debts and possessions.

Grace breathed the scent of sandalwood, mingling with an aroma of fire-cooked food from outside the tent. She had not eaten for hours, and even her tense state of nerves could not blunt the edge on her hunger. Her hand swept the beaded curtain to one side and she entered the lounging area of the tent. The blue glass lamps held on brass chains made a soft blue twilight, beneath which stood the crescent-shaped divan, the stools of red leather, the low tables silvered with arabesques.

The blue light played over Grace as she stood there, silent and tense, and up to her ankles in the deep pile of the magnificent carpet that covered the floor. It was all shades of topaz and gold, like the desert itself, while the saddlecloth slung across the divan was like a flame.

The wish that she might hate the appointments of this tent flared through her, but her senses betrayed her and she couldn't suppress her admiration of the carpets, the hangings, the craftsmanship she saw in the oriental furniture. She hated the man even as she admired his taste, and she found herself drawn towards a glass-fronted bureau in a corner of the room.

It was superbly lacquered with peacocks and minarets, the desk section closed and locked — for she tried the flap. Above the desk, behind the little panes of glass, was an assortment of books. There was a row of novels, a few of them with English titles, several with French authors, and others in Persian and Hebrew. Again the fact that he was educated was more of an affront to Grace than if he had been a truly wild son of the desert, who knew no better than to give in to his caprices. She frowned and saw that the remainder of the books were on travel, animal care, falconry, lion hunting, horses, and archery. A collection of books that might have belonged to a gentleman who cared only about the outdoor life ... but her own presence here told Grace that Kharim Khan indulged in pursuits other than those of a horseman and a hunter.

She was standing there, gazing at the books, and feeling curiously struck by the name of one of the authors that appeared on several of the travel books, when a faint sound touched her ears, and her very nerves.

She spun round and stared at the man who stood just inside the tent, framed against the blue wall of it, clad in black cloth trousers clipped at the ankles, topped by the pale, almost armoured gleam of a thick silk tunic, deeply open at the throat. He was clean-shaven, and the hard, sculptured look of his features was both fascinating and terrifying. His eyes were a deep, brilliant green, lambent as a leopard's in the blue light of the hanging lamps. His hair, uncovered, was raven dark, cut close to his well-shaped head, with the sheen of an eagle's wing to it.

For a stunning moment he seemed a stranger ... the Kharim Khan she had known had been bearded, but this man was shaven ... recently shaven, for the paleness of his chin and jaw contrasted with the bronzing of his upper features.

Her blue eyes clashed with his green eyes, and she knew him in the very depths of her being.

His eyes swept over her, from head to toe, missing not an item of the dove-coloured dress, the frame of the collar, the white belt about her slim waist, her right hand clenched in the deep pocket in the folds of the skirt.

'*Quel puritain,*' he drawled.

'*Quel vilain!*' she shot back at him, an amethyst blaze to her eyes, for it was as if Satan himself were standing there, a black and silver devil, with sinful green eyes.

'So that is what we are, eh? The sinner and the saint.' A smile of pure mockery gleamed in his eyes as he advanced into the tent, making no sound on the tawny carpet. 'I hope, little saint, that for all your angelic looks you have an appetite for the supper Achmed is about to bring to us. I believe he has excelled himself in our honour, so if you will be seated, Theldja—'

'Don't you dare to give me one of your outlandish desert names,' she flared. 'It's insult enough to be *here!*'

'But the name suits you.' His voice matched his dangerous flicker of a smile, a slight almost cruel movement of his mouth, aided and abetted by a taunting glint in his eyes. 'What is more astonishing and terrible in the eyes of a man than a woman of ice-cool purity? "*She who looketh forth at dawn. Fair as the moon. Clear as the sun. Terrible as an army with banners.*" Those words were attributed to Solomon, and he was very wise, they say.'

'He was Solomon,' she said cuttingly, 'and you are Kharim Khan. I prefer to be addressed by my married name!'

'But you no longer have a marriage, Lady Wilde. A chapter of your life has closed, and here in the *Dasht-i-Sheb* another begins. However, the name Wilde is evocative of other lines written by a man not quite so wise or revered. Later on I shall quote them, but not right now.' He gestured with his right hand and the ring upon it gleamed, rather like a malevolent eye. 'You will notice that I have books, that I read, that I know English authors. Are you not impressed that the barbarian has an intellectual side to him?'

'Quite frankly, it makes you more of a monster.' Grace tilted her Tillerton chin at Kharim Khan and was defiant enough in this moment not to care if he completely lost his temper with her. That he had a strong, quick temper was apparent in every supple line of him. He was alert, fearless, cunning and swift as a leopard, she was sure of that. His face, shorn of that dark beard, reminded her of a bronze mask she had once been shown in an Egyptian museum ... that of the Moon-God Sin, who was part of ancient legend and said to be reborn in human form each passing of a half-thousand years.

Tonight in the turquoise tent Grace was strung to a pitch so nervous that she could well believe anything. Back at Reza Shahr everyone had said that the Persian desert was a strange place, and right now she could feel that strangeness as tangibly as she could smell the spicy scent emitted by the hanging lamps in which cassia oil was burned. It seemed to rise to her head, so that suddenly she had to sit down on the divan, or find herself in an ignominious heap at the *khan's* feet. She battled with the dizziness and knew that it had a lot to do with her physical hunger.

The aroma of food revived her, for in that moment Achmed appeared with the supper tray, which he placed on a table at the side of the divan.

Supper? It was a veritable feast, consisting of rice and

breast of partridge served on silver plates filigreed with birds of paradise. Roasted flesh of gazelle with various vegetables baked in the succulent gravy; barley sprouts, potatoes, carrots and tiny onions. Honey tarts were followed by peaches, which in turn were followed by a fragrant coffee brought to them in a silver service, this time incised with running gazelle and leopards.

Grace had eaten the food in a kind of hungry spell, aware of the subtle taste of herbs, the delectable aroma and taste of the gravy in which the bird, meat, and vegetables were cooked. The honey tarts melted in her mouth, and the tang of the peaches was just right, as was the coffee, being neither too sweet nor too thick, as it had been served at Reza Shahr.

The hot, satisfying, tasty meal did wonders for Grace's morale, and she was able to sit back and relax with her second cup of coffee, the delicate silver shape of it lined with palest porcelain. The saucer depicting a gazelle in flight from a leopard . . . such appropriate insignia, which she felt sure amused the *khan*.

He sat not close to her, but at the other end of the crescent-shaped divan, his long legs crossed as he lounged back against the scarlet saddlecloth. He, too, had eaten his food with hunger, using his fingers to eat the partridge, and then surprising her by switching to a knife and fork to eat the gazelle meat and the vegetables.

'When Achmed returns to take the coffee service, you will oblige me by thanking him for such an excellent meal. My Persians are less hard-centred than I. They appreciate a word of thanks.'

'I shall be only too pleased to thank Achmed for such a delicious meal. He is a superb cook – much finer than the Ambassador's chef at Reza Shahr. Naturally you would acquire the very best for yourself, Kharim Khan. Your pride and arrogance demand to be fed and pleasured by only the best.'

'I am glad to see that you are back in form after wilting a little,' he drawled. 'Even Persian honey tarts have not sweetened your sharp tongue, milady. They are a harem dessert, by the way.' His smile was indescribably wicked. 'I noticed that you thoroughly enjoyed them.'

'I knew perfectly well the origin of the tarts,' she said sharply. 'On my previous visit to Persia I was a *visitor* at the house of a wealthy Persian and I spent an afternoon with his women, being shown some of their "secrets". I had tea with them and honey tarts were served.'

'I noticed how you emphasize that on that occasion you were a visitor.' He gave her a lazily amused look as his hand stretched to a silver box and took from it one of his dark slim cheroots. 'Don't you regard yourself as a guest of the Haklyt Rohim?'

'A guest, Kharim Khan, is invited to a residence, not brought there against her will, so don't try your subtle oriental game of twisting facts to put yourself in the right and me in the wrong. At no time did I willingly choose to come here . . . I was forced into compliance and I am your prisoner, not your guest.'

'You know, milady,' he blew a small cloud of smoke whose strong tang mingled with the aroma of coffee and cassia oil, 'we have a saying that Destiny is written in letters of gold and black. In all situations there is a bright side, and a dark side, and you may find that within a few days you are a captive of the desert rather than my prisoner. I recall how your eyes shone, the morning that we set out from Reza Shahr to seek the desert of Sheba. From the moment you set forth on that journey, Destiny was riding at your side, and it was she, not I, who whipped up a sandstorm, who cut you loose from a man you had already grown to despise—'

'I knew you were listening outside my tent that night,' she said tensely, with accusing eyes fixed upon his bronzed face. 'I imagine it greatly amused you to hear what Tony said, and did. I am sure you are a man who thinks the pride of women should be slapped out of them, until they grovel at your knees and plead for mercy. If you have that kind of picture in your mind with regard to me—'

'My lady,' he drawled, 'the picture I have in mind of you

98

is not one of hurt dignity and the mark of fingers across your cheek. You really must put out of your mind the belief that all men resort to brutal measures in order to have their way with a defeated, crushed, weeping woman. Such an image of desire certainly does nothing to arouse my blood. *Et alors?* Come, you must agree that I have made no attempt whatsoever to crush out the fire that flashes between us so agreeably, and excitingly. I have been since a very young boy an admirer of the spirited filly, and the creature closest in temperament to the filly is a woman of sleek fighting beauty, with nostrils tensed to every scent in the air, with wide eyes that seek and search, with long slim legs with speed in them, with a glow to her, a swift pride and a certain reserve.'

'Yes,' she flashed, 'I've noticed that you treat women as if they are wild ponies to be tamed. I should have mentioned before that your little *kadin*, Shalena, is really lovely, though obviously trained to obey your slightest wish. But do you think it quite kind to send her to wait on your – your newest acquisition?

There was a tiny, taut silence after Grace finished speaking, and then to her annoyance the *khan* flung back his dark head and filled the blue tent with his laughter. She saw the sinews stand out like cords of gold silk in his throat, and the neck of his tunic opened wider to reveal the muscles of his upper chest, the dark spread of hair, and meshed in it the golden amulet of Fatima's Hand on a gold chain.

He had a barbaric attraction, a supple strength, a lazy mocking air of a leopard stretched across her path to freedom, and to be laughed at by him was almost more than Grace could endure.

'You certainly do live by your own rules,' she said cuttingly. 'I thought Persians were at least respectful of their own women, even if they do like them well trained in obedience.'

'You amuse me, but truly.' The wanton laughter still played and lurked in his green eyes. 'My lady, the young girl Shalena has been betrothed to my manservant Achmed since she was a child of seven. Soon they will be married, here in the desert, and I beg of you not to ever say to anyone else of the Haklyt Rohim what you have just said to me. I do indeed respect Persian women, and I most certainly would never take for my passing amusement a betrothed girl. It might amuse you to imagine a knife in my back, but it would not be a joke I could laugh at. The Persian male has a strong arm and a long blade to his knife, and believe it or not, my heart is not made of stone.'

Grace stared at the empty coffee cup in her hand, and hated it that she had made a fool of herself by accusing him of being Shalena's lover. She felt the hot colour come into her face as the mortifying thought struck her that he might suppose she was jealous of the Persian girl. The relief was acute when the flap of the tent parted to admit Achmed, who came to take away the coffee service.

Grace's cheeks were still flushed when she raised her eyes to the olive-skinned Achmed, who looked almost double the age of Shalena, and thanked him in Persian for the supper she had thoroughly enjoyed. 'I have never tasted better, Achmed.' There was a guilty rush of warmth in her voice. 'You have a great gift for making food taste heavenly.'

'It is my pleasure that my lady is pleased by my humble efforts.' He smiled, half shyly, and cast a swift glance at the *khan* for his confirmation that the meal had been praiseworthy.

'You may cook for the gods, Achmed, when I have ceased to require earthly nourishment.' Kharim Khan smiled, but without a play of mockery in his eyes. 'I see that you have brought nuts and sweets, so we shall not require anything further tonight. You have worked well, so feel free now to enjoy the company of the pretty Shalena.'

Achmed gave a bow, first to the *khan*, then to Grace, and withdrew in his silent way from the tent, closing the silken flap carefully behind him.

The silence within the tent was somehow intensified by the sound of a Persian song carried to them from the fires where members of the Haklyt Rohim would be grouped to enjoy their relaxation at the end of the day. The song came ebbing and flowing on the little gusts of night wind blowing in the desert. The vast, silent, starlit desert . . . a sphinx who could be as spellbinding as she could be cruel.

'We are the lovers of the desert.' The *khan* spoke reflectively. 'We court her, we delight in her, we fight with her, and now and again we sing to her. But never is she to be subdued, and that is why she is our favourite mistress. Love is no passive emotion. It has many moods, many facets to it, a promise and a mystery never fully realized. We chase it like a shadow, we clasp but a dream. We are given the pleasure of an unforgettable night, or an unbelievable dawn, only that we might endure an intolerable day. And yet even so a desert day can surprise us by sending a soft cloud of rain through which we ride, soul and senses cooled to the verge of bliss, skin and eyes soaking in the freshness, lungs and throat gulping in the air as if it were a ripe wine released from the springs of the earth itself.'

As he spoke a green fire played in the depths of his eyes, as if he were never more happy than when he could gallop through the desert cooled by those tempestuous bursts of rain that were over all too swiftly. 'It is a primitive and wonderful experience, to ride so, and after the rainfall come showers of wild flowers in the *wadis*, coming alive out of the dust and stones, more aching with colour than the jewels of the Queen of Sheba herself.'

Then with a shrug, as if he knew that Grace was not receptive to his words, he leaned forward and took a handful of nuts from the divided silver container on the divan table, which also held wild cranberries and tiny golden plums, and a selection of sweets.

'Come, help yourself to berries, or a piece of that inviting candy.' A sardonic note had returned to his deep voice. 'I have these in place of wine, for my people are true to their religion and I eat as they eat, and drink coffee or goat milk as they do.'

'How big of you to make such a sacrifice,' she said freezingly. 'But quite frankly I can't see you in a hair-shirt. You obviously prefer silk, and the other fine things of life. Look at the carpets you tread upon – they're priceless! And I'm sure that chess set is worth a king's ransom.'

'Indeed it is, *chérie*, but it will not be used to ransom even a *khan*.' As he used that endearment – which sent a little snake of alarm slithering up and down her spine – he tossed an almond into his mouth and his teeth showed white as he chewed the nut with lazy appreciation. 'All that I possess is really the possession of the Haklyt Rohim. If they ever needed the help of money, these things would be sold, but not otherwise. Yes, each carpet is beautiful, but in each one a part of the pattern has been flawed so that the eye of evil won't fall upon perfection. The devil craves to destroy or corrupt what is perfect.'

'I'm well aware of that!' She looked at him with eyes like blue ice, letting him know that she thought him a devil . . . out to destroy her body and soul.

A smile glittered in his eyes as he took her meaning, and he made no denial of her implication. With his lashes half lowered, so that the shadows of them darkened and made almost menacing the emerald gleam of his eyes, he deliberately studied her as she sat in her grey silk against the scarlet covering of the divan. He seemed to stroke her golden hair with his gaze, to fondle without touching the pallor of her slim throat within the shield of her Quaker collar, to run a caress all the way down her slender body to her fine-boned ankles.

'I thought you a rare creature when I saw you at—' he paused, almost imperceptibly, 'Reza Shahr. My judgment is borne out a hundredfold when I see you in the setting of my tent. Here you are "*Whitely wanton with a velvet brow. A mouth like a pomegranate cut with a knife of ivory*." The man who wrote those lines – perhaps to a woman, perhaps to a boy – had your surname, Lady Wilde. He might well have had your image in his brilliant, strangely romantic mind. In breeches and shirt, with your hair partly concealed, you look a boy who might tempt a satyr. In your silk, *mon puritain*, you look a woman to tempt a saint. And as I see from the ice that glitters in your eyes you do not regard me as a saint, so the temptation I feel must be very devilish, eh?'

'You know your feelings, I know mine,' she flung at him, fingernails curling at the sides of her dress as if she longed to reach out and rip his face. 'I despise your compliments and everything about you. The girl Shalena believes the lie you have told your people – that as a widow I am under your protection. I – I would sooner trust the protection of a grizzly bear! At least I wouldn't have to listen to shameful flattery, and sanctimonious talk about the sacrifices you'd make for your tribe! You're a decadent, spoiled, amorous and amoral man, without a scrap of mercy, or a dash of conscience. You're so accustomed to reaching out for women as you reach out for a nut or a sweet, that you've lost all sense of guilt ... if you ever had a sense of guilt about anything!'

'I really cannot remember.' He stroked his shaven chin and looked mockingly reflective. 'Um – as you say you prefer the grizzly bear, perhaps I should have kept my beard instead of dispensing with it. However, we have plenty of time for it to grow again, if you would like that?'

'You – you know what I'd like – I have money. Won't you let me pay for my release?' She hadn't meant to plead with him, but the words were suddenly stronger than her pride and wouldn't be held back.

'I, too, have money,' he rejoined, and his narrowed gaze dwelt on her lips, as if he knew what it had cost her to make her plea. 'Does it not make a change, my lady, to be with a man who actually sees *you* and isn't blinded by your bank account? Surely the feeling must be a novel one? I would say that for most of your growing up you felt not unlike a slave who knew she would be bargained for in the marriage market of European society. It was never a secret from you, I am sure, that you were expected to pay with your person for the privilege of being an heiress.'

'And it would seem,' she said icily, 'that I am never to cease "paying with my person", as you put it! If you don't want my bank account, then you must want me! Well, in that society you are so scornful of, I was married by the man, not snatched away to a desert tent to be treated like a – a *kadin*!'

'You seem fascinated by that word,' he drawled. 'It is rather more attractive than concubine, or kept woman, is it not?'

From ice she went to fury . . . of its own accord her right hand leapt forward, fingernails flying for his lean, mocking, distinctive face. She wanted to claw him, to mark him, to have a primitive moment of release from her pent-up emotions of the past few days. But he was as quick as she and before she could stab her nails into his cheek he had hold of her wrist and was gripping it until she felt her bones would snap.

'Quick-tempered as the sand-cat, aren't you?' His eyes were alive with devilry as his other arm snaked about her and with a strength that was utterly frightening jerked her to him and held her in a captive embrace on the divan. It was true to say that she had never felt so helpless in her life . . . each bone in her body seemed aware that it was in danger of being broken . . . each nerve beneath the surface of her skin was in acute panic as she was forced into close contact with the warm, supple, ruthless body of Kharim Khan.

The age-old phrases of panic, and real virgin fear were on her lips and would have found expression had he not spoken again, using words that aroused her pride and made cries and pleading the craven way to behave with this man.

'Well, my virgin with the amorous mouth, how will you tear out my eyes when I have you like this? You know well enough that I could break you in two . . . look at your eyes and how they give you away! Yes, I could break you, in body and spirit, but being a perverse man, and one who likes the half-broken filly rather more than the one who accepts the halter, I am not going to use brute force on you.' He laughed softly, so that his warm, smoky breath stirred across her lips and her eyelids. 'A man should dominate you, otherwise you would become too proud, but he should never make you completely submissive. Is the moon submissive? Is the sun, or any other of the elements? It is part of their beauty that they are controlled only by the tides; only by the winds. My soul! What should I want with a slave at my knee? A creature afraid of me? A passive toy for my pleasure? Theldja, do I look a man who likes what is tame?'

'You look a devil!' she flung in his face. 'A mocking, cruel devil, and if you refer to me by that name again—'

'But, my child,' he mocked, 'it is merely the Eastern name for snow. A quite lovely name, for a commodity we often only see on the peaks of the mountains out of our reach. The very first time I saw you I thought to myself how like a being of snow you were; how cool and distant, how white-skinned, with your eyes like the blue sky above the snow, your mouth as red as the berries that grow in the snow, and your hair like a glistening swathe of sunlight. At once, like a knife striking, I wanted you here in the desert. It seemed to me that only in the desert would you melt into a warm, alive, responsive human being.'

'I suppose the fact that I had a husband meant no more to you than a fly to be flicked out of your way?' she said dis-dainfully.

'You had no husband the first time I saw you. It was in a Persian garden, by a pool where the wide-open lotus were fooled by the big golden moon. You had drifted out from the house, where a wedding party was going on, and you never knew how close you came to being cloaked and carried off. I held my hand that time . . . but when the opportunity came a second time I did not resist the temptation.'

'You were at that Persian wedding?' Her eyes wildly searched his face. 'I remember there were tribesmen there – that they rode in from the desert on marvellous horses, their harness all hung with silver pieces and blue beads. You were one of those men?'

'Indeed. The bridegroom was of the Haklyt Rohim. You don't recall everything, of course. You were but a girl, diz-zied by all the strange rituals, the feasting and the music, the many people present. A Persian wedding can seem like a feast of tigers, I will admit.' A smile quirked on his lips, but his hands still held her with that relentless promise of bruising strength. Her impulse was to be free of his hands, but her instincts warned her that if she struggled he would inevitably master her struggles and in the process she would find herself completely subdued. It was better to remain still, to let him talk of the wedding, at which she did recall those big, somehow ferocious men moving with lean, hard grace in their robes among the more sedately dressed city guests. She had been confused by it all . . . yet, looking at him now, she was struck by a recollection of the tall, robed figure who had approached the bride on her dais, clad like an idol in her finery and her crown of pearls, painted and almost unnaturally still among all the activity. That man had presented the girl with a gift, Grace remembered, and the bride's mother, proud and smiling beside her daughter, had accepted it for the girl . . . who had to remain as if like an idol until her bridegroom came for her. There had been an avid eagerness in the mother's kohled eyes, and Grace had wondered what the gift was. Then, even as she had wondered, the musicians had started to play again, and she had suddenly slipped away beneath one of the arches, into the moonlit garden. There in the depths of the garden, out of range of the wailing music, she had in a while heard a man singing . . . of the forces of destiny.

*Kismet. Mektoub.* It is written!

Grace, whose destiny had seemed always ruled by her grandfather, was now aware of new forces in her life. An invisible deity named Fate, and another who was far from being intangible, for he was unbearably close to her . . . his strength, his sun-gold warmth of skin, his gaze that seemed to penetrate her mind, were all too real, too vivid, to be dismissed ever again as a frightening dream from which she must awake in due course.

She was wearied by all that she had gone through, but she had never felt more awake in her life. More aware of sound and texture and the tang of tobacco on the warm skin of a man. She was caught, held body and gaze by him, like a bird trapped by the paw of a cat. He had the dark good looks of a pagan, an audacious sweep to his brows, deep sun-lines cleft into his skin, and lips that took the striking curve of a scimitar. When bearded he had looked more fierce ... but clean-shaven he showed a chin as firm and obstinate as the grip of his hands.

'When,' she asked, for she had to know; the slight weight of the tiny gun in her dress prodded her into knowing, 'will you let me go?'

The jade eyes narrowed until the lashes met, and his scrutiny of her hair, her skin, her lips was cruelly explicit. 'The guest is impatient of leaving even before she has enjoyed the full extent of my hospitality?' he drawled. 'I should be less than the perfect host if I did not insist that you stay – a while.'

'And how long is that, Kharim Khan?' She strove to speak calmly, and not to let the awful, rising panic back into her voice.

'A night, perhaps. A week, *chérie*. Or maybe a year.'

'Don't play with me! Don't taunt me – tell me!'

'Do I really have to put it into words?' And with a soft laugh, as deceptive as the purr of a leopard, he suddenly lowered his face and buried his lips against the fine gold hair at her temple. 'Tonight is not yet over, and no man of the East presumes to know what the dawn will bring.'

# CHAPTER SEVEN

THE kiss he pressed to her temple was, somehow, more shattering than the expected savagery of a kiss upon the mouth. And combined with his whispered words it put Grace into such a spin that she could no longer remain like a statue in his arms. She had sworn to herself that she would not be touched by him again, and now his touch became like a flame that suddenly engulfed her, so that with a cry she wrenched herself away from him and felt the pain as her wrist was bruised by his fingers, and her body flayed by the iron-like muscles in his arm.

'I hate your touch ... and despise you ... and wish it were you who lay dead in the sand!' Her eyes blazed blue fury at him, so maddened was she by his whisper that the night was not yet over. 'Take your hands off me ... take them off before I scream down this camp and let your people know you for what you are ... a brute and a rapist!'

'What an eloquent tongue you have for a titled lady,' he taunted. 'But don't you think you go a little too far? A brute is lacking in reason, and I had several reasons for bringing you here. A brute is callous and without feeling, and I do assure you that I have many feelings when I study the unusual beauty of your face. It is true that I have carried you off, but can you really say that I have deprived you of your chastity?'

'You've made threats—'

'Threats, my lady, are not deeds.'

'You know as well as I—'

'What do I know?'

'Why you've brought me here.' There was anger, scorn and trepidation in her eyes beneath the soft cloud of hair that had fallen across her brow in her struggle with him. If only she could break free of his grip, but he was so strong and he didn't care about hurting her. 'I – I'm not an innocent schoolgirl. I'm married – I know what men are, and what sort of feelings they have towards women. None of you really care beyond your own gratifications!'

'The men in your life have really taught you to hate the male sex, have they not?' He studied her pale face with the anguished mouth for several moments, and his own eyes were unfathomable, as they could be when he wished it so. Green and hard as gems, and not even mocking her as they raked over her features, which had the pride and the privacy of a person whose heart had never been really touched by another human being. Only Grace alone knew that she wasn't a cold and passionless person, but she had learned to keep people at a distance. She had become adept at guarding her true self ... and as she felt the *khan* seeking out her secret self with his disconcerting eyes, the resentment of him, and the terror, rose in her like a scream for help.

Her mouth opened to let free that scream, but instantly his hand had freed her wrist and was flung across her lips, choking off her cry that would have echoed through the tent into the night around them, where his people sat and talked and were unaware, or unmoved, by the plight of a mere woman.

'None of that nonsense,' he said curtly. 'Surely you are woman enough to accept what has happened to you without betraying your dignity? No one will help you, for it will merely be assumed that you are grieving for your husband.' His hand slid away from her mouth until his lean hard fingers were enclosing her slim throat; he tilted back her head until her eyes were filled with his face in the blue light of the hanging lamps.

'My lady, I won't have my people believe that you grieve so desperately for a man who betrayed you with other women; who was so petty and shallow that he preferred the jangle of glass beads to the shimmer of the pearl. Accept that you are here, for it will be much better for your nervous system if you do acquiesce. Let yourself submit to the fact that I do prefer the precious gem to the specious glitter of the painted toy.'

'You — you can have no sense of right or wrong,' she whispered, for his fingers as they toyed with her throat made her feel as if she might faint. 'You can't just *steal* a woman and hope to get away with it. The authorities will search for Tony — for me.'

'And they may find a grave,' he agreed. 'Or they may not. At night the desert winds blow and the sands shift and all traces of a passing caravan are smoothed away, as if by a giant hand. The desert is the eternal sphinx because she never reveals her secrets. She is the one woman who sees all and speaks not a word. *Insh-allah.*'

'My God, it's a blasphemy to call this the will of Allah,' she said witheringly.

'Was it any better what you did, my lady? You stood in a church and made vows of love for a man for whom you felt nothing. You walked a lamb to the altar and allowed yourself to be sacrificed to a loveless marriage. Having stood once in the slave market, why so much objection this time? Is it because I am Persian?'

'I — I wouldn't care if you were Turkestan! I object to having my life interfered with — my freedom curtailed — my person manhandled!'

'I see.' The mockery crept back into his eyes. 'So the marriage to Lord Wilde was more suitable for you than a marriage founded on emotion. It provided you with the freedom to keep your heart to yourself, and your body, not to mention your soul. Love unlocks the heart, does it not? Love uncovers the body. Love enslaves the soul.'

'What would you know of love?' Anger ran in her veins again, and her lips curled red against her white skin. 'You surely have the words mixed up. It's lust you're talking about!'

'Is it indeed?' His eyes filled with that cruel amusement that seemed to turn her blood to ice, and leaning closer to her he made her aware of every bone and sinew in his masculine body. 'And shall I now turn out the lamps, my lady pure, and teach you that even *you* are capable of lust and its total, mindless pleasure? Shall I strip you to your ice-bound soul and make you a slave to my slightest wish or whim? I can do it, Theldja. I can take you, and so break you to my hand that you would only be alive in my arms, wanting nothing and no one but me, night and day. It wouldn't even matter if you hated me, for you would still want me. So shall I teach you about lust, so that I might accuse you of living for that and nothing else?'

His words were shocking, not only in their context, but because Grace knew in that moment that he was unbearably close to carrying out his terrible threat. She had met women, seen women at society parties who were so enthralled by a certain man that they were like beautiful, blind sleep-walkers, going through the motions of living out the day so that they might spend the night in the arms of a lover who left them with bruises they covered with silk and bracelets, and the off-key laughter of women doomed to be deserted. And from desertion they went from hand to hand . . . unable to love, and yet unable to stop giving themselves.

A shudder she could not suppress swept her body. 'May I have a drop of water?' she asked faintly. 'I feel – I don't feel quite well.'

'I am sure you don't,' he said dryly. 'You must watch your words, *mon ange*, or my temper may lose itself.' And so saying he withdrew his arm from around her and pressed her back against the divan. Then he rose to his feet and went through the beaded partition into the inner room, where Grace had noticed earlier the flagon of water and the tumbler on the bedside table. As the beads rattled and then left a moment of silence, Grace jumped to her own feet and in a desperate hurry she dragged from the pocket of her dress the chiffon handkerchief in which her tiny gun was folded. When her fingers clasped the pearl handle, a surge of relief ran through her. He who considered that he knew everything had not known about the gun . . . Grace compressed her lips and tensed her spine . . . he had raised hell in her heart, and if he still refused to give her an escort out of this encampment, then she would use the gun and he would learn what it felt like to be helpless and terrified.

When the *maille* rattled again, Grace felt keenly the presence of every nerve in her body. She stood there, the little gun poised and steady in her hand. The fear had passed, and a kind of recklessness had taken possession of her. It was there in her eyes as she flung back the hair from her brow, a shimmering defiance, as of a gambler playing her final card and not quite certain if her opponent held a trump.

Her blue, defiant eyes fixed themselves upon the tall figure of Kharim Khan, who had adopted the instant stillness of a leopard when it scents danger. In his hand was the tumbler half filled with water, and the water was absolutely steady, without a bubble to blur its clarity.

Grace had known in advance that the man was nerveless, but a taut thread of irritation tightened within her that he should not reveal by a flicker of an eyelid that she disturbed his self-assurance by holding a gun to his chest.

'I want to leave this place,' she said firmly. 'I want to leave tonight, and you will provide an escort to take me to Reza Shahr. If you do this, I shall say nothing about being abducted by you. I shall forget the incident.'

'I see.' The glass of water still remained absolutely without movement in his hand, yet there emanated from his lean, hard body a wave of power that made Grace's fingers tighten upon the gun. She would be unafraid to us it, for she was Grace Tillerton Wilde, and the derring-do and ruthless will of Jonas were in the marrow of her shapely bones. It was the unpredictable, subtle and supple movement from the *khan* that she waited for, and her every nerve was tensed and ready for that movement.

'The gun looks a pretty toy,' he murmured, 'but I am sure you know how to use it.'

'Did you think me such a blind innocent, Kharim Khan, that I would travel in the Persian desert without some sort of protection from the men I would be travelling with?' Her mouth was scornful. 'I never learned about affection from my grandfather, but I learned other, far more useful things. I was tutored by an expert in the uses of a gun, and I have always been an avid pupil. I know exactly the position of your heart, *mon ami*, and being a person, as you said yourself, to whom men have not been kind, I would feel no regret at putting a bullet through your very fine body. It would be like shooting down a leopard in my path, for men . . . men mean nothing to me.'

'I am sure you believe every word that you say.' His voice was cool, his gaze as steady as the glass in his hand. 'Unfortunately I cannot give you what you ask for . . . tomorrow the Haklyt Rohim move northward to cooler, greener pasture, and each man expects to travel with his family. Even for you, my lady, I will not disappoint a man of my tribe.'

'Even if it means that I shall kill you?' she asked. 'When you are dead in the sand you won't be able to feel the cool air on your skin, or to see greener pastures . . . even though the *Qur'an* teaches that men of your faith shall finish in paradise. Your paradise is down here on earth, on a fine horse riding in the rain, or in the warm arms of a woman. I have only to press the trigger of this pretty toy, as you call it, and everything will go cold and dark for you, and you will see no more wild flowers in the desert, and no more pearls against the skin of a woman. You know it and I know it, for you're an educated man, and you probably read the *Qur'an* for the stories it contains rather than the divine promises. Am I correct?'

'You are a little fool,' he drawled, 'if you think you can frighten me with your threats.'

'I am not making threats.' Her eyes were diamond-blue as she levelled the little gun at his heart. 'If you won't set me free, then what have I to lose if I pull this trigger?'

'You prefer the mercy of my men to me?' He arched an eyebrow. 'I am flattered, for it probably means that I have aroused more emotion in you, my lady, than has been aroused by any other man. I am sure you would only have winged Lord Wilde, but you really mean to end my life, don't you?'

Grace stared at him, and suddenly it struck her that he had known all along that she possessed the gun. She tried wildly to recall the words she and Tony had flung at each other, the night they had quarrelled. She caught her breath, almost as if she heard Tony's voice again, and the note of panic in it: 'Put that thing down, or it will go off in a minute!' To someone listening outside the tent, those words would have betrayed the presence of a gun inside the tent . . . a gun she held, and therefore owned, and would have with her, here in the encampment of the Haklyt Rohim.

'You enjoy taking chances, don't you?' she flung at the *khan*. 'Perhaps you imagined that I was a novice when it came to firing a gun. I do assure you that I'm not, and that was why Tony was so afraid.'

'Do you imagine that I'm afraid?' A smile flickered on the *khan*'s lips. 'I have seen a hungry hawk bring down a running gazelle, so I know to what lengths a desperate creature will go. I am quite sure that you would like to bring me down, but I am not running, Lady Wilde, nor am I giving you escort back to your – friends.'

'Why?' she demanded. 'Have you loaded my gun with blanks? Is that why you're being so brave?'

'My lady, what an acid little tongue you have! Did no one ever teach you that honey will get you further with a man than vinegar will?'

'To the devil with placating, beguiling and seducing men!' she returned, with a toss of her head. 'In my experience they aren't worth the bother. Men live to please themselves, and they think that women live for the same purpose. Not me! Not again, ever!'

'You say it with such passion,' he drawled, 'as if you really mean it.'

'What typical male arrogance to assume that I don't mean it.' A sudden memory stabbed at her, of a youthful, bygone attempt to win some tenderness from Jonas, which he had only rebuffed. Her eyes clouded over . . . and an instant later shot wide open as cold water was flung directly in her face, blinding her as the *khan* leapt forward and with a chopping movement of his hand knocked the gun from her hand.

Shock, pain . . . the two sensations made her reel, while the water ran down her face and soaked through the silk of her dress. The action had been unbelievably swift and accurate, and totally unexpected, that a man should throw water full in her face . . . in her eyes, her hair, and in a stream down the neck of her dress.

'And that, *mon ange*, should cool some of your bitter passion for a while.' As he spoke he bent to retrieve the gun from the floor, and as Grace blinked the water from her eyes she saw him approach the bureau in a corner of the tent, unlock the writing-flap and place the weapon in a small compartment of the desk. He then turned to her, and though he appeared to have the key in the palm of his hand, when he showed his hand the key was gone.

'You tricky devil!' she flung at him, nursing her wrist. 'Brute!'

'And what are you, my fine lady?' He mocked with glittering eyes her bedraggled appearance. 'An immaculate angel to wave a loaded gun at my person and threaten to put a bullet in my heart? Did you really imagine that I was going to remain a standing target for you? I like too much to be alive, and furthermore, you wouldn't enjoy the desert justice of my people if you took my life. As you are under my protection, their anger would be extremely fierce.'

'Protection?' Something between a laugh and a sob escaped from her throat. 'Is that what you call it? In my language it's sheer, wanton, unforgivable abduction. Why, your men saw you throw me across your shoulder! Was that a sign that I was your willing victim?'

'No, merely a sign of a tantrum, or a little weariness of the legs.'

'You smooth liar!' Her voice shook as she felt the bruised bones of her wrist and saw the dark marks spreading against her skin. Her life seemed to be made up of men who used force against her, and the pain and the accusation were in her eyes, as the ruthlessness was in the hard set of his mouth. *Tendresse* was something to which Grace had long been a stranger . . . but suddenly, like some Victorian maiden in a novel, she found herself shrinking away from the *khan*'s powerful male body. He couldn't know, for no one knew, that she had been a wife in name only. She had never divulged her secret, and felt convinced that Tony had never said a word, and now she was deadly afraid of this man of the desert, whom she had angered beyond the point of forgiveness.

As the fear stabbed at her heart, she gave way to it and turning blindly to the *maille* of beads she thrust through it into the interior room ... the *chambre à coucher* ... running further into the trap like a vixen pursued.

Only a single lighted lamp burned there, making soft shadows that played over the furnishings and the embroidered faces in the tapestry at the head of the bed. Grace glanced round wildly, seeking the escape that was not possible from the other part of the tent, where the *khan* was stationed like a transcending figure of doom and vengeance. She ran into the alcove where she had bathed, but there was no exit from there ... and yet there had to be, for these tents opened at either end, for the admittance of servants with bath water, and for the purpose of cleaning and tidying without disturbing the *khan* if he was taking his relaxation in the main area of the tent.

Grace closed her eyes a moment and fought down her panic. When she opened them again she knew that the exit was in the harem, for it was from there that Shalena had slipped away, avoiding the lounging area. She had gone like a shadow, as if walking through a wall, and the walls in the bedroom were hung with tapestries that could very easily hide the rear opening of the blue tent.

Silent-footed on the carpets, Grace hastened into the bedroom, where she took stock of the shape of it and decided that the way out lay behind a softly gleaming purple silk hanging. She swept it to one side and to her joy felt the flap that opened to the night outside. Her hands shook as she pushed the flap aside and slipped through the opening into the cool darkness ... only to cry out as she blundered into the hard figure of a man.

Strong hands caught at her, and laughter purred in a deep throat.

'*Mon ange*, I am too seasoned a hunter not to guess which way my quarry will run.' And so saying he lifted her into his arms, and her legs had gone so nerveless that she couldn't stop him; she was the running gazelle brought down by a hawk, and when he laid her down on the bed and she felt his hands at the belt of her dress, all she could do was shiver with distress, and give a little protesting moan as his hand slid round to the side of her waist, where her dress was fastened.

'W-what are you doing?'

'Removing your damp clothing – being your valet, as I don't wish to have a sick girl on my hands in the morning, when camp is struck and we set out for Mahnaz, as glowing and entrancing as its moon name, with high plateaus of rock and in between deep swards of grassland. You will wish to ride and not be carried in a litter, so off with the dress – so! And this slip—'

'No!' She thrust aside his hand and looked at him with eyes huge with indignation, her hair madly tousled from his forceful removal of her dress. 'Leave me – please leave me a little dignity—'

'Dignity and a desert chill do not go hand in hand, and I have learned already that I can't trust you to be left alone.' The silk made a whipping sound as her slip was removed in one brisk movement, and as with a shamed cry she rolled over on the dark fur coverlet and concealed herself, the *khan* strode into the bathing alcove and returned with one of the huge, fuzzy towels. He wrapped Grace into it, using force because he had to, and he proceeded to rub her down as if she had been a favoured filly who was in a froth after a mad chase over the desert hills.

One part of Grace's conscious self said that it just couldn't be happening ... the more physical part of her knew that it was happening. The slight, fine curves of her body felt the brisk pressure of the masculine hands through the towel, rubbing her skin until she glowed and ached and begged for mercy.

'I'm not – oh, for heaven's sake – I'm not *your horse!*' she cried out, and at that he threw back his dark head and the *chambre à coucher* rang with his laughter. And when he ceased laughing, he ceased his towelling and suddenly bent above her, so that she was pressed to the fur, with only the towel between her bareness and the silk tunic covering his broad chest.

'Not my horse, but my woman, Theldja. Now the name just has to be yours, for never in my life did I see a woman with a skin so like snow to look upon . . . so like warm milk to touch.'

Trapped . . . fearful . . . even a little fascinated, Grace was held by the jade-green eyes that roved her face, her throat, her white shoulders against the dark and glossy fur. A strange languor seemed to be stealing over her, as if the leopard eyes were stealing the fight and the courage right out of her body. As the handsome head came lower, as the warm breath stirred across her face, she found the will-power to turn her face away from him. The frightened heart beat wild wings inside her, there in her breast crushed to his body.

'Come,' he murmured the word against her averted cheek. 'You deserve a taste of the whip, my little filly, rather than a petting – but come, why be shy with me any more? I know how beautiful you are, and you know that I don't intend to let you go. Be kissed instead of bruised. It is far more pleasant, for you, and for me.'

'Really?' She spoke in a muffled voice. 'I should have thought that you thoroughly enjoyed being unpleasant to me—' And there she broke off with a gasp as his lips ran their warmth across the side of her neck and downwards to the curve of her shoulder. The caress was the greatest intimacy she had yet received from a man, and her body tautened as if a lash had been applied to her. She felt the warm, firm lips travelling into the curve of her arm, and instantly, instinctively, her fingers crooked into talons and raked upwards into the nape of his neck. She clawed him with all the desperation of a little animal, finding with her female instincts one of the most vulnerable parts of the human male.

'*Quelle diable*!' He flung her painfully away from him and surged to his feet. His face in the lamplight was savage and his eyes were ablaze with pain and temper. 'You really are a vicious young creature ... as fiercely defendant of your virtue as any Persian virgin! *En effet*, what have you to lose ... you, the wife of a man such as Wilde ... a known rake-hell?'

Each word had a curt, cutting sting ... the contempt, the certainty that she could be no better than the man she had married, was suddenly too much to endure, and the hot, painful tears flooded into Grace's eyes and set them shimmering with an awful loveliness and despair.

The *khan* stood above her, there at the side of the wide ottoman, and he stared downwards as the tears rolled down her white cheeks. These were not tears of temper, but the tears of a deep, heartfelt anguish, stored up in her for months ... years ... spilling molten across her lips to her throat, shining in the lamplight.

Abruptly the *khan* knelt upon the bed and watched the silent tears that pearled from her eyes and melted against her skin.

Outside in the night the desert had grown very still. The camp fires had smouldered into smoke and the men had drifted to their tents. Just now and then was the silence broken by the soft clang of a camel bell, or by the distant yap of a jackal.

'You cry, my lady – for him?'

'No—' Her despair was too deep for the defence of a lie. 'I never loved him.'

'You were his wife.'

'I was married to him, but I was never – his.'

'You were a wife in but name?'

'Yes.'

A deep, lengthy silence followed her words, and then she heard a faint click and a few seconds later breathed the smoke of a cheroot. She let her lashes remain closed against her cheeks, captured and held by the tears she had cried. She felt the give of the ottoman as the *khan* rose to his feet. Though his footfalls were silenced by the carpet, she sensed that he didn't leave the room. He seemed to take only a few paces away from her, and then he was back, and leaning over her.

'Come, put this on,' he murmured. 'You cannot lie there in a towel like an infant – though it would seem that you are now *mon enfant* rather than *ma belle*.'

Grace had never heard him speak with such soft humour before, and so she opened her eyes to look at him, her lashes wet-spiked about the pink lids of her eyes. The savagery was gone from his face and his expression was quizzical as he handed her the nightdress which Shalena had laid out for her. 'I'll turn my back,' he drawled. 'If I must!'

Grace's fingers gripped the silk nightdress and her gaze followed him all the way to the *maille* of beads, where he paused and let forth a stream of smoke from his cheroot ... then the beads rattled and he was gone. Still she didn't move, until suddenly a cool breath of air stirred across her bare shoulders and the realization struck through her that she was all but naked.

Aroused from the lethargy into which her fit of weeping had sunk her, she flung off the big towel and slipped hastily into her nightdress. Then, in the grip of a weary resolution not to weep or beg ever again, she got into the bed and lay under the silk sheets and the fur throwover, hating the nervous tremors that shook her every few seconds.

She was lying there, her face buried against her bare arm, when she heard the beaded curtain give entrance to the *khan*. She had to clench her teeth in order not to cry out to him not to touch her – please! She sensed rather than heard him come to the side of the ottoman.

'Look at me,' he said. 'I know you are not asleep.'

She turned her head and stared up at him, and her face seemed filled with her great blue eyes. He towered beside the bed, and he wore his great cloak, a corner of it flung over his broad shoulder. 'I am going to ride camp,' he said quietly, 'to ensure that all is well and the guards are posted at their positions. The Haklyt Rohim are not without their enemies, and tomorrow is a big day for all of us. Sleep deep, for you must be awake with the dawn.'

Then – miraculously – he was gone, striding away in his tall boots, with his night-blue cloak wrapped about his tall figure. He left her in the dimly lit harem quite alone, but it was many minutes before her body and limbs finally relaxed, before a warmth stole over her, and she fell into the embrace of a slumber that proved to be as dreamless as it was deep.

When Grace awoke she felt slightly dazed from the depths of the sleep into which she had been dropped by her exhausted emotions of last night. She knew exactly where she was, for this tent and its appointments would be indelibly printed upon her mind to the end of her days, but she just couldn't shake off her residue of sleepiness, and almost unaware she rolled over in the bed and buried her sleepy head in the unused part of the huge, silk-covered pillow. She was dimly aware that she must rouse herself, but she felt so reluctant to face the day that lay ahead of her. To wake up completely was to realize that she was no longer free to do as she pleased. Whether she liked it or not she was 'a woman snatched', and by a man who had so far proved that he could outwit her.

Her arm flung itself across the silk surface of the pillow and bruises showed dark against her skin; her fingernails dug into the silk as if they would rip it ... and then they tensed as she caught the sound of someone entering the *chambre à coucher*.

'*Bonjour, madame.*' The girlish voice of Shalena spoke at the side of the bed. 'I bring coffee for you, *lella*.'

Grace turned her head and opened her eyes; her lips moved in a faint smile and as she sat up she pushed the tumbled hair from her blue eyes that were still a little heavy from her storm of weeping last night. Then, as she accepted the cup of coffee with a murmur of thanks, she noticed that Shalena was gazing inquisitively at the indentation of a head left in the pillow at Grace's side. Uncontrollably a flush ran over her face, for she knew to what conclusion the girl jumped, and she inwardly cursed herself for rolling all over the bed and making it look as if two people had shared it.

'Have I time for a bath before,' Grace gulped a mouthful of hot, aromatic coffee, 'before camp is struck and we – we move on?'

It was awful to have to endure what the girl obviously thought . . . Grace wanted to deny it, but who would believe her? Now that she was more awake, and her eyes were avoiding a direct meeting with Shalena's, she saw the evidence that the *khan* had been into the harem while she slept. There on the stool at the foot of the bed was flung the tunic and trousers he had worn last night; a stubbed cheroot lay in the ashtray at the right side of the bed and there still hung in the air the tang of his cheroot smoke.

Her hands clenched on the coffee cup as she visualized him looking at her while she slept and was unaware of his scrutiny. Everything he did seemed an invasion of her privacy . . . he had even exposed her to the belief that she was his mistress . . . he had meant to make her so, and then had lost interest – for the time being – in a weeping heap of misery. That was all that his abrupt show of gallantry amounted to! He was accustomed to a willing response to his ardour and didn't like having it damped by a storm of tears.

'Would Madame mind cold water for the bath?' Shalena asked tentatively. 'Already tents are being struck and the animals assembled, and it would take time to heat the water—'

'A cold bath will suit me perfectly,' Grace said at once, and she welcomed the idea of a cold plunge that would not only refresh her body but her mind as well. She had learned that with Kharim Khan she had to keep her wits about her. She finished her coffee and handed the cup to Shalena, who ran her gaze over the bruises on Grace's arm and then glanced away.

'I will go and fetch the water, *lella*.' There was a breathless note of sympathy in her voice, and then she was gone with a tinkle of ankle chains . . . a young and pretty girl who had known from an early age that she was to be married to a man double her age, but a kind man who would treat her with a kind of reverence because she was but a girl, slim and honey-skinned, with the big, slanting brown eyes of a doe.

Grace sat for a long moment staring at the *khan*'s clothing slung across the stool near the end of the ottoman. A picture rushed into her mind of how he had stood there last night, clad in the great cloak that increased his look of ruthless male power. She bit her lip as she recalled the slight smile curling on his lip, as if he were contemptuous not only of her tears but her fear of his maleness. *Mon enfant*, he had called her, but through the words had run a steel-fine thread of warning that he would teach her, before very long, to become a woman.

As if the memory struck her like the flick of a lash, Grace leapt from the bed and dragging her robe around her, searched her suitcase for a plain linen shirt to wear with her breeches and boots. To be clad in the garb of a boy was some kind of armour against the *khan*. A jaunty, delusive protection for her body, even if her mind could not forget the vulnerable, shivering piece of womanhood he had dealt with last night.

To escape that shameful image she hastened into the bathing alcove, with her shirt, breeches and fresh underclothing clutched in her hands. She was there when Shalena entered with a blue water-jar, followed by another woman who gave Grace a quick, shy look. Grace, gathering the old poise around her as if it were a cloak, murmured the Persian greeting and pinned up her hair as the two women began to fill the bath, making several trips with the beautiful water-jars with slender necks. The two Persian woman were like Ruth and Naomi coming back and forth from the well, their feet bare and brown, the soles painted with henna, above which the anklets of finely chased silver made a soft, sensuous music.

By the time the bath was filled Grace was chatting to them in their own language, but she sensed that they were both a little in awe of her . . . to each of them she was the *khan*'s woman. They addressed her as *lella* which meant lady, and not for one second, and for this she was grateful, did they treat her as if her presence in the *khan*'s tent cheapened her in any way.

Their manner plainly informed her that she was honoured, even if Shalena had looked rather askance at the bruises inflicted upon her by the *agha* . . . their lord and master.

When the bath was ready she informed Shalena that she would manage alone and not trouble her any further. 'You must take a little rest after your exertions,' she smiled. 'I shall be fine.'

'You will take breakfast with my lord?' the girl asked.

Grace's heart seemed to plummet. 'I – I expect so,' she said. 'Where is he right now? Do you know?'

'With the men, *madame*, giving them their instructions.' Shalena broke suddenly into a vivid smile and her dark eyes sparkled. 'It will be wonderful to be at Mahnaz again, and this time I, too, shall be living at the palace, for tomorrow night, *lella*, I am to be married, and when we arrive at Mahnaz I shall dwell with Achmed.'

'The palace?' Grace echoed. 'I don't understand—'

'Has my lord not yet told you?' the girl asked. 'His palace of residence is at Mahnaz, and it is a very beautiful place. My lady might prefer it to a tent . . . as she is not desert born. I am desert born and so I shall be married in the desert. I hope my lady will attend?'

'I shall like that, Shalena.' Grace summoned a warm note to her voice, but at heart she felt cold and apprehensive. So at Mahnaz the *khan* lived in a palace, and such a place had large doors with heavy locks on them, and rooms where an Englishwoman could be kept for as long as he wished to keep her.

Shalena paused a moment before leaving the alcove. 'I feel sure the *lella* will find much at Mahnaz to admire. The home of the *ahga* is known as the Palace of the Pomegranate.'

Silence followed Shalena's departure from the alcove, but while Grace took her bath the sounds of activity increased beyond the walls of the blue tent. The encampment was now alive with people making ready to be on the move, mustering their goods and chattels, their children and animals for the long trek to summer pasturage. The black tents were being struck and corded on the backs of the camels. The donkeys were being laden with rolled rugs and bedding, cooking pots and sacks of provisions, the looms on which clothing and curtains were woven, not to mention the smaller livestock bundled into sling-pouches.

The excited voices drifted to Grace, and then her nerves tightened as in the lounge of the blue tent she caught the deep voice of the *khan*, answered by Achmed, and the tang of coffee as it was poured. Grace tucked her shirt into the waistband of her breeches, and stamped her feet into her boots, and her every nerve felt keyed up for further conflict with the *khan*. She would not be carried off to his palace with the outlandish name! She would not tolerate this situation any further!

The bead curtain rattled as she pushed it to one side, and as she stepped into the presence of the *khan* she could feel the furious beating of her heart. He glanced up from where he sprawled on the divan, a cup of coffee in his hand, and on the table at his side a tray of food. 'Bonjour.' He rose in one lithe movement to his feet and gestured with his free hand to the divan. 'Achmed has just brought breakfast for us. You slept well? There were no undue disturbances?'

He might have been the perfect host inquiring of his guest that all was well with her, but Grace caught the flicker of amusement in his eyes and she knew to what he referred when he spoke about disturbances. Her temper quickened, and her sense of injustice at being played with like a pawn in a game of chance. Everything about him was an outrage to the independence she had valued, and which even Tony had not truly denied.

'Good morning,' she said coolly, and it was her natural need for food which led her to the divan, where she sat on the very edge in her cream-coloured breeches and tailored blue shirt. She bided her time before broaching the subject of the palace, and when he gestured that she help herself she proceeded to do so. She poured a cup of the smoky, fragrant coffee took a slice of the hot cheesecake stuffed with sultanas and a couple of slices of meat, buttered a knob of the dark crunchy bread, and ate her breakfast as if it didn't disturb her at all to have seated nearby a large, lazily amused, hawk-faced man, clad all in white but for his jackboots of a darkly gleaming ox-blood colour.

This morning he ate adroitly with his fingers, tossing the food into his mouth as if to emphasize the fact that he was desert bred and not in the mood to impress his lady guest with his good manners. But of course, she amended to herself, it was the accepted manner of eating for a man of the East, and she could only marvel at the way he kept his robes so impeccably spotless.

'You would like to ask me a dozen questions, but you just don't know how to begin,' he said, and when her blue eyes flashed to his face, the dent at the corner of his mouth deepened. '*Encore une tasse*, to help you find the courage?'

'I don't need to find the courage to speak my mind to you,' she said witheringly. 'You think yourself so clever, don't you? You are so sure you see into my mind as if it were a crystal ball!'

'I have the oriental facility for "eating the thoughts" of another person, I do admit.' with suave courtesy he lifted the coffee pot and refilled her cup. 'Try some of the melon jam, or perhaps a pomegranate. They are unusual with their golden skins, but they come from the garden of my palace at Mahnaz.'

'The Palace of the Pomegranate!' she snapped.

'Quite so.' He leaned back and looked at her, lazily ready to enjoy the tantrum which was building up inside her. 'You like the name?'

'Isn't it a trifle outrageous and pretentious for a prison?' She glared at him in his desert robes and jackboots. 'You people have a saying, "Let the guest command the host", but you don't abide by it, do you?'

'And what would you command of me, milady?' He reached for one of the golden-skinned pomegranates, held it a moment between his hands, and then broke it apart as if imparting a subtle threat. Watching her, he bit into the fruit with his white teeth, and as he chewed the pink flesh she thought again of a leopard stretched at its ease and yet alert to every movement, every sound, every scent. He was menace personified . . . and he knew . . . yes, he knew of the terror that quivered inside her as his gaze roved the curve of fair hair above her eyes and took in the clarity of her bones under the flawless pallor of her skin.

'End this cruel sport,' she said tensely. 'Allow me to go before . . . before it becomes degrading. You're a proud man—'

' "I am not a foe",' he quoted. ' "Do not fly me as the lamb flies the wolf, or a dove the hawk." '

' "It is for *love* I pursue you." ' Grace concluded the lines in her mind, for he was speaking of the pursuit of Daphne by Apollo. The virgin Daphne who ran crying a prayer that she elude him, and was turned into a bay tree.

'How pale you are!' He dipped his fingers into the small bowl of water at the side of his plate and wiped them on the snowy napkin. He lifted the napkin. 'Almost this colour, *petite*, as if I drain the blood from your heart. But lovely! Akin to pearls and milk and the finest silk. Will you stab me with bays if I touch you?'

'I – I shall stab you at the first opportunity – if you insist on making me stay with you.'

'Will you really, my little girl who has not yet learned what it is to be a woman?' he laughed at her. 'Then we shall both be guilty of *une crime passionnelle*, shall we not? And how will your angelic nature bear with that, I wonder, for every act of passion has love or hate involved, and you would have me believe that you are not a creature of earthly feelings. *Mon dieu*, what heaven on earth if you were, after all, a thing of flame instead of ice! I wonder, though,' he abruptly reached a hand to her cheek and before she knew it he had stroked his fingers down her face to the point of her chin, 'I feel the warm blood under your skin, not the ice-water of the frozen virgin. And I see the warm blood paint the fine skin over your cheekbones. You really are – intriguing.'

'Don't,' she spoke tensely, 'pay me compliments. I don't want them!'

'Then you are a rare creature,' he drawled. 'Women usually grab at compliments as they snatch at jewels, and how provocative our kind of jewellery would be against your pale skin – the barbaric in contrast to the civilized, eh?'

'It is barbarous of you to keep me with you when you know—' Her fingers clenched her table napkin. 'I won't come with you! I won't be dragged along to your Palace of the Pomegranate as if I were something from a – a slave market!'

'*Ma belle*, how you exaggerate.' He stretched his arms, flexing his wide shoulders under the sweep of his robes. 'I shall not be dragging you to the palace by your hair, and how can you speak of being treated like a slave? Naturally I don't expect you to accept this situation *sans aucune plainte*, but accept it you must. It has happened that you are with me. It is a fact. What, after all, have you to go back to? After a suitable delay another marriage arranged for you by your grandfather, to another spoiled creature you would probably despise much more than you despise me. At least I take you for yourself. For your proud, high-tempered valiance . . . and for the way you sit a horse! *Bien!* You don't roll in the saddle like a suet pudding, but you sit straight and firm like a young cavalry lance. I like that, Theldja. I like that very much, as I value my horses. Thoroughbreds can be wrecked by mishandling.'

As the *khan* spoke these words he looked directly into Grace's eyes and she knew that he referred to her. That thread of panic ran through her, knotting in her midriff, an actual, physical jag of feeling that made her press a hand to her side. This, combined with the dominance of his gaze, made her drop her own gaze to the deep cleft in his strong obstinate chin. A rift in a rock, into which the tip of her forefinger would have fitted.

Suddenly she gave a start as something landed on the divan at her side. She stared at it and saw that it winked and gleamed. 'Pick it up,' he ordered. 'It isn't a *gage d'amour*, but let us call it a trinket the exact colour of your angry eyes, in that ivory white skin.'

'I don't want slave payment,' she flared. 'Keep it!'

'All I have had from you so far,' he mocked, 'is temper, high-toned scorn, and a flood of tears. I would hardly reward you for those, my lady. Now pick up the jewel and fasten it to your shirt – or shall I perform the operation for you?'

She scowled at him, but when he moved slightly, as if about to carry out his threat, she took hold of the jewel he had tossed to her, and then found herself staring at it in startled fascination. It was a small mask pendant in gold, ivory, opals and turquoise. Tiny golden snakes formed the headdress of the mask, the eyes were of turquoise, the face of ivory, and from below the chin hung a fire opal on a tiny gold chain. It fastened with a golden pin, and never in her life had Grace seen so perfect a piece of jewellery, and so unusual that it caught at once at her imagination.

'Why do you give it to me?' she murmured.

'As a small recompense, let us say.' He rose to his feet, and as always in his robes he seemed taller than ever, towering above her as she sat on the divan, gazing in a reluctant admiration at his gift.

She glanced up at him. 'Is it some kind of an amulet? I see that you wear the Hand of Fatima yourself.'

'All desert people are superstitious,' he said. 'There is a kind of magic in gems, but the mask reminds me of you. Ivory face, eyes the sky-colour of the turquoise, fire in your temper like the opal, and gold in your hair. But wear it as an

amulet if that will make it more acceptable to you. Furthermore, it is too bizarre to be acceptable to a *kadin,* if you are
curious on that score. The oriental girl prefers her adorn-
ment to be more traditional . . . as you may have noticed in
Shalena. The mask pendant is *you,* if you understand
me?'

'Yes – I understand you.' And for the first time he had
shaken her belief that she was just a desert barbarian, lawless
and wilful, and unconcerned about her feelings. Her fingers
shook a fraction as she pinned the pendant to the collar of
her shirt, where it blended against the blue material and
hung its fire opal just above her heart. Then she stood up
and raised her eyes to the *khan*'s face. 'Will it protect me
against you?' she asked.

The hint of sternness fled from his lips and the mocking
quirk took its place again. 'The turquoise is said to prevent a
fall,' he drawled. 'It could imply a fall from grace, eh?'

'You always have the answer, don't you?' She tilted her
chin as she looked at him, and thrust her hands, with their
slight but annoying tremor, into the hip pockets of her
breeches.

'You invariably have the question,' he rejoined, sweeping
his gaze over the boyish stance she had assumed. 'I think you
would like me to believe you an intellectual woman, which is
nonsense! The roots of your being run deep beneath the
layers of ice, self-imposed reserve, and distrust of men.
When with a thrust I bring them to the surface, they take
fire too swiftly to be emotions ruled by your intellect. I am
not saying you are not a clever young woman, but you aren't
guided by the natural cool reasoning of a cerebral person.'

He paused there, and his eyes narrowed to a gleaming
jade. 'You are cold in the way some passionate people
become after a disillusionment or a bitterness . . . and I look
forward, *petite,* to seeing what the desert does to you.'

Her hands clenched in her pockets. 'So you have no intention of releasing me?' Her words sounded quiet, but her
heart was thumping beneath her blue shirt. She felt so furi-
ously helpless when she looked at the *khan,* his booted feet

planted firmly in the rugs, a powerful and picturesque figure of a man, who had assumed ruthless control over her life, her person, her future!

'Jailer!' she flung at him. 'You're no more than that! And if your towering ego imagines that I'm going to be captivated by your desert palace, then you're in for a disappointment. Anywhere that you are is no place where I want to be. I'm not honoured or flattered by your attentions. You personify all that I find arrogant, selfish, bullying and brutal in the male of the species. Neither you nor your desert will ever charm my eyes or melt my heart. I'm pure marble where you're concerned!'

'Exquisite marble,' he drawled, and deliberately reaching out a hand he touched the pendant on her lapel, fingering the fire opal and letting her feel the hard warmth of his fingers against her breast. She tautened as if a viper touched her and was about to sting her, and she saw the slow, mockingly cruel little smile play about his lips.

'If you harbour the faint hope, my lady, that one of my people will be bribed into helping you get away, then you also are in for a disappointment. I have the complete loyalty of the Haklyt Rohim, apart from which they are desert people with strong but simple needs, which, in their eyes, I share. It is right for a man to have a woman to share his tent, and that you share mine makes you sacrosanct. Do you understand me? Each man knows that if he assisted you in any way to leave me, then I would be justified in applying desert law to punish him. He would, you see, be guilty of running off with my woman, and I am the *khan* of the tribe. As the desert is old so are its laws. As the desert can be ruthless so can its punishments. So, Theldja, if you value the lives of others, forget any scheme you might have for securing an escort out of my reach. My reach is long, and my justice has to be tough, for I rule a desert toughened tribe of people. For one of my men to ride off with you would be tantamount to rape . . .'

And as she caught her breath at the word, his hand suddenly wrapped itself about the slim, vulnerable nape of her neck, and he held her like that, her shocked blue eyes looking up into his, her bright hair streaming over his fingers.

'The word has gone round the camp that last night you lay with me, and because on a long journey it is customary for a man to take a temporary wife in everyone's eyes you are now my "wife" and the Persian laws regarding a wife are fearfully strong. Much more so than in your own country, among your own people. If I caught you with another man I would not only have the right to punish him, but I would be justified in punishing you – and you are a sensitive creature, for all your talk of being marble. Your white skin bruises easily, and you can be hurt to an exquisite degree.'

He stared down into her eyes, and it was as if a flame licked over her as the black pupils expanded against the jade-green irises of his eyes.

'Don't make me hurt you, Theldja. Be warned that my temper is as strong as my admiration for your exquisite face and body. Marble?' He laughed softly. 'How little you know yourself!'

He then let her go and swung to the flap of the tent. 'Go pack your belongings. It is almost time for us to leave, and the men must strike my tent and load my camels.'

His order hung in the air as he departed from the tent, and Grace stood indecisive, biting her lip, still feeling his touch on her skin, still swept by a storm of rebellion against all he had said to her.

His woman! His temporary *wife*! His property, labelled with an awful punishment if any one of his tribesmen dared to accept a bribe from her in exchange for her freedom.

She felt enraged by her own sense of helplessness. Every particle of common sense told her that it was useless to attempt to ride off across the desert without an escort. Even if she grabbed a mount and got away without being seen, she would soon find herself hopelessly lost in the Persian desert ... at the mercy of something even more terrible than the *khan* himself.

Her fingers crept to the mask pendant that winked and gleamed against her shirt.

He had a few human feelings ... but the hot, gold, sprawling desert had none. A person lost there would hear no human voice, only the shattering of sandstone in the fierce heat and the burning stillness.

# CHAPTER EIGHT

GRACE learned on that trek to Mahnaz that the *khan* and his people worshipped the sun almost like pagans. They revelled in its fierce caress and seemed capable of travelling even longer distances a day than Kharim Khan permitted. The children grew dark as young hawks, and Grace learned to tear the fire-baked bread with hungry hands and to mop up the meat and rice stew without spilling gravy all down her breeches. Inwardly she felt rather proud of herself for the way she stood up to the trek ... and it was also a stunning relief that whenever the night fell and the hay-stuffed mattresses were stretched beneath the blazing stars, the *khan* made no demand of any sort upon her.

She would gaze at the stars and be amazed by how near they seemed ... she would feel the vigilant green eyes upon her, the alertness emanating from that lean, sprawled body ... she was still very much his prisoner, though he didn't touch her.

The desert all around them was her cage of gold ... the sheer spaciousness of the desert at night both fascinated her and alarmed her. And she was never really sure when the *khan* slept, and when he lay awake; all she knew was that he had the ability to relax like a great, sleek cat, and she sensed that he would spring after her if she made any attempt to creep off in the night. It was her fear of this, of suddenly finding herself an actual captive in his lean brown hands, that kept her chained to her desert bed.

She wasn't sure of the strength of the leash on this man who was so darkly bronzed in the sun, so lambent-eyed in the starlight. All she knew was that sinews in her stomach would tighten in a strange, electrical way at his slightest movement in the night. Her fingers would dig into the straw mattress, her nerves would churn, and in her imagination she would feel herself drawn into his arms of bronze and any cry she might make would be silenced by his bold and mocking lips.

It was always a breathless relief when daybreak came, breaking open the dark sky with vivid streaks of violet and orange. Then for a short while a passionate dawn beauty held sway over the desert, until suddenly the sun sprang alive and brazen in the sky, rejuvenated after the abandon of its dying the night before.

One morning a rainfall brought flowers alive in the desert, a carpet of purple and scarlet which would last but a day or two and then be shrivelled to dust by the hot wind. As the rain fell the *khan* slapped the neck of her horse, his green gaze blinded her eyes for a moment, and then his teeth flashed in a vivid smile as he invited her to gallop with him in the rain.

Grace's long scarlet cloak blew in the wind above the hindquarters of her mount as she and Kharim Khan raced across the sands that turned from gold to brown as the rain lashed down and blew in their faces. Her nostrils were filled with the wild, almost animal smell of the wet sand as they galloped madly, side by side, as if racing towards an invisible goal.

When the rain finally ceased, they came to a halt, and their eyes fought a silent battle as they faced each other from the saddles of their prancing mounts. The sting of the desert rain had made her eyes glow, and the white headdress she was wearing was an attractive, foreign frame for her blue eyes carved at a jewel-like angle in her wind-flushed face.

'Now admit that you enjoyed every moment of that,' he said.

Her eyes followed the rise and flick of his whip in the air, and she was acutely aware of the black wing of his cloak blowing about him, adding to his look of barbaric splendour in the saddle of his pure-bred stallion of rain-washed metal-grey. The two together were like figures of fierce beauty, sprung from an antique canvas painted by a master. They were etched against the blue-grey sky like carvings in teak and metal.

'Glorious,' she murmured. 'Your desert has its moments, *seigneur*.'

She had fallen into the habit of addressing him so. The appellation not only suited him, but somehow it kept him, if only in her mind, at a certain distance. It told him that she had no intention of calling him Kharim ... it seemed aeons ago since she had thought of him as her guide and had casually addressed him by his first name.

As she sat there, and the wind-freshened air blew about them, she had to endure the searching of his eyes all over her. Here in the desert she had succumbed to the oriental headwear that was more endurable in the sun than a hat, which seemed to tighten about the head in the heat. The scarlet burnous appealed to her sense of beauty, which she could not suppress or deny, and as she saw the tensing of the *khan*'s nostrils she realized that his own sense of beauty was affected. It would have been foolish of her, unrealistic and coy, to have pretended that she wasn't aware of her good looks ... the fair and damnable attractiveness which had landed her in her present predicament.

'In desert apparel your beauty is even more English,' he said. 'And yet there is a hint, a secret glow of sensuality beneath the coolness, rather like a fountain in a walled garden, concealed by the cool shadows, yet there and beckoning. Already you are coming alive in the desert ... more alive than you have ever been, deny it though you will.'

That night when they struck camp, and after supper had been consumed and the plates and cups carried away by Achmed, Grace became aware of a certain restlessness in the *khan*'s manner and this set beating fast a pulse in her throat. As he prowled about the fire of shrub and tamarisk, creating smoke of his own with a dark cheroot clamped between his teeth, Grace sat tense with her arms locked about her breeched knees, half afraid to look at him in case she caught his gaze upon her. Her mind became filled with images of that wild gallop through the rain, and the look he had passed over her at the end of it.

He was a man of intense masculinity, and the entire encampment looked upon her as the *khan's lella*. He prowled, like a leopard, she thought, with a leash upon him which tonight seemed stretched to its limits.

Later, beneath the diamond fire of the stars, as he stretched out upon his straw mattress, he called to her: '*Bonsoir, mon enfant*,' and there was in his deep voice a note of irony. Grace rolled over and buried her face in the cushion of her own bed, and it seemed incredible that he was being *chivalresque* . . . this man of the desert who had grown up to dominate and to take what he fancied.

*Mon enfant*. He had called her so the night he had learned that her marriage to Tony had never been a realistic one, and here under the desert stars she lay in a kind of mental and physical torment, her fair hair tousled on the cushion, the sheepskin cover twisted off her slim body that ached from the long hours on horseback. Grace lay only yards from the lean, brown, supple body of the *khan* . . . who had snatched a woman for himself and found her to be a virgin.

The following morning the Haklyt Rohim struck an awesome, waterless mile upon mile of unrelieved desert of bright yellow sand, glaring to the eye, and even as Grace inwardly shrank from the thought of crossing it, the *khan* rode to the side of her mount and informed her that this was the final stretch of barren desert before they reached the foot of the mountains.

'Tonight we shall camp in the lap of the hills,' he said, scanning the horizon with his keen eyes. 'And you know, of course, that tonight Shalena becomes a bride. You look forward to this, I hope, for you will be attending the ceremony and the feast that will take place afterwards.'

It was neither invitation nor request, but a direct order. Grace, however, had grown fond of Shalena and she had no intention of not attending the girl's wedding. She knew herself secretly excited by the thought of seeing a desert wedding, and she gave Kharim Khan a slightly amused look.

'Did you imagine you'd have to force me to attend?' she asked. 'Shalena has already requested that I go, and she has been good enough to show me her dress and the jewellery she'll be wearing. I'm quite human with people I like, you know.'

'There is no need to remind me,' he drawled, keeping his mount in step with hers as the mile-long caravan of the Haklyt Rohim began to cross the yellow sand. 'So this will be your second Persian wedding, eh? But this time a desert one and rather more — romantic, lit by the stars and the dancing fires, between a couple who are very, very fond of each other. Achmed is a fine fellow, and he will see to it that his young wife is cared for and much loved. And we have a belief that a couple who take vows in the desert are blessed by the passionate forces of the wind, the sun, and the stars. In fact people of the desert are called the children of the stars.'

'That's rather beautiful,' she admitted. 'Having been born in the desert, *seigneur*, you are a child of the stars.'

'Oh, very much so,' he agreed dryly. 'I have the winds and the wilds in my veins and actually dislike sleeping under a roof.'

'Then it will please you about as much as it will please me to be under the roof of your palace. Why are you returning there if you dislike having a roof over your head?'

'It is my headquarters and every so often I am expected to be there in order to hold meetings with other heads of the clans. Also it is close to the summer pasturage of my people, and there are one or two courts of justice I must hold. You look at me in such a questioning way, *petite*. Are you thinking that I am a bad example of justice to my tribe?'

'Aren't you?' she said. 'You know, even if your people only suspect, that I am not with you from choice.'

'You are with me because Fate willed it that way.' A smile of faint irony flickered on his lips. 'I didn't ask to be enchanted by your face in a Persian garden. I didn't expect to ever see you again when you left with your grandfather. When you returned, the strange forces of Fate began to play tricks with both of us.'

'You were the one playing the tricks,' she rejoined. 'Pretending to be a guide—'

'You didn't have to believe that I was one,' he mocked. 'Several times I caught you looking at me in a doubtful way, as if something about me struck you as being less obsequious than you expected. That was why it so pleased you to call me a servant – your instincts told you that I wasn't one, but you distrust your instincts in case they betray you into being a woman of heart instead of a creature of marble. By denying your instinct concerning me, you played into my hands. I am almost tempted to wonder if your secret self, the self you deny, played deliberately into my hands.'

'What an absurd idea,' she scoffed. 'As if I'd choose to be your prisoner, even subconsciously! What are you trying to do? Relieve your conscience of its burden of guilt by saying that I'm secretly thrilled to be with you, classed as your *kadin*, made to endure hours of desert travel, subjected to a straw bed at night, and given only a jug of water each day to wash in? My God! I'd have to be crazy, wouldn't I, to want that kind of existence! Or madly in love! And I hope I'm suffering from neither of those heat-strokes!'

'There is one thing Theldja,' he gave his deep, purring laugh, 'you rarely suffer from a lack of vocabulary. Most Persians, you know, consider the joy of their life to be a serene and silent woman.'

'Most Persians, *seigneur*, are sensible enough to refrain from kidnapping an English woman. We are too emancipated to enjoy *purdah*, nor are we taught from an early age all the tricks to please a man. I am sure I must be a singular let-down for you, but you're too obstinate – only once before in my life have I seen a chin as obstinate as yours – to admit defeat and let me go. What do you plan for me at the Palace of the Pomegranate? Am I to disappear, like the disappointing ladies of the *seraglio*, into some deep lake in a weighted sack?'

'*Mon dieu*, what an imagination you do have!' A glint of ironic amusement came into the green eyes beneath the black, slashing eyebrows. 'Can't you think of something more pleasant for a man to have planned for a woman of your rare charms?'

Grace knew at once what he implied, and her grip so tightened on the bridle of her mount that the chestnut balked, flung up on his heels, and would have unseated her if she had not been expert enough to keep her seat as she controlled the mettlesome young horse.

'Settle down, Beauty.' That was the name she had given him. 'Forgive my bad manners! I know you're a gentleman, don't I?'

She heard a whiplash of a laugh, and after Beauty had settled into his stride again, she rode along in silence, hoping to be left alone; praying that the *khan* would gallop away from her side and join his young *aide-de-camp*, a Persian of considerable good looks, who sometimes shared supper with them and played chess with Kharim Khan.

'Did I ever tell you about my great-grandmother?' he said suddenly. 'It's a story you might find interesting.'

'I – I'm not interested in your antecedents,' she rejoined. 'Nor in your present relations. Why should I be? They can only regard me as your creature, for it's what you've made everyone believe me to be. You have been clever at that! Even Davoud Sayed looks at me at times with a sly little gleam in those black-almond eyes of his. Is he hoping that when you're finished with me I shall be passed on to him for a while?'

'That is a remark fit only for the back alleys of a grimy city,' he said cuttingly.

'Manchester?' she inquired. 'That is where my ancestors were bred and born. As a boy my grandfather wore hob-nailed boots and ran errands for those with a shiny brass knocker on the front door, and a servant or two in the kitchen. I'm really no lady born, *seigneur*. It's no real distinction to have stolen me from among the ladies of society. If my grandfather had not made a fortune out of people's greed for candy bars and wrapped toffee, I'd probably be working in a cotton-mill or assisting in a High Street tea-

shop. If I lack the basic refinements then you must blame it
on my lack of blue blood. Unlike yourself I don't come from
a long line of ruling *khans*, and you must excuse me if I
don't comprehend the arrogance which permits you to ride
roughshod over my freedom, my feelings, and my future. I
see only presumption in your action, and feel about as
honoured as a street girl hired for the night!'

'You won't speak in that way!' Now his eyes were blazing
into hers, the lazy, almost inquisitive amusement wiped out
of them, leaving only the vivid, flashing green. 'I won't
permit such talk from you! You have been treated with
every respect by the Haklyt Rohim. My people think of you
as my ward!'

'But I am not your ward, Kharim Khan! I am the widow
of Lord Wilde, and you've made me feel like a kept
woman!'

'Yes, you are kept.' His white teeth snapped on the words.
'But you are more of a child than a woman. You are treated
by me like a daughter, and you know it, so don't talk of
street girls and dishonour. You know nothing of that side of
life, and I won't hear again such things from your lips.'

His own lips as he spoke were curiously ashen against his
deeply tanned skin, and Grace stared at him a moment
before turning her gaze to the hot yellow sands, clouding up
about the horses and camels, and the plodding donkeys
laden with their motley of pots, bundles and small children.

That strange feeling of not really knowing this man at all
swept over her, a curious chill of a feeling running over her
sun-hot skin. This was one of those occasions when he made
her feel deeply afraid of him . . . and at the same time re-
luctantly in awe of him. He always seemed quite a youthful
man to be in sole charge of so many desert people, but when
he showed his authority, it was truly a formidable sight . . . a
lightning in his eyes, a deep thunder in his voice, with an
edge of steel to it.

Because he made her feel afraid of him . . . in awe of him
. . . she had to defy such feelings.

'Would you be so chivalrous in your attitude if you hadn't a Moslem fear of violating a virgin outside the bonds of real marriage?' she taunted him. 'It's the sword of Damocles above the Persian head, isn't it? You have me, but you haven't!'

'Be quiet, you little shrew!' And as he spoke he leaned forward from his saddle and Grace winced as the tip of his riding whip flicked across her shoulder, leaving a sting across her skin, and a sudden smarting in her eyes. The yellow desert wavered like the ocean itself as she stared at it through her tears, and she felt, rather than saw, the swerving away of the *khan*'s horse, leaving an abrupt emptiness at her side. Her lips quivered. She hated him . . . hated him! He was brutal, proud, and furious with her.

Suddenly she raised her own whip and flicked the coat of her mount, who being unused to the whip leapt angrily forward, and then bolted like a red streak of lightning across the livid sands.

Grace had often sensed the speed there would be in Beauty if he was ever allowed a free rein . . . now he had taken it, grabbed the initiative, and was off like the thoroughbred that he was, racing the wind of the desert with Grace crouched low in the saddle, a trifle scared at first, and then all at once exhilarated as she realized that she was speeding away from the *khan* and might elude him if she was lucky.

Her red cloak billowed and the landscape fled by in a dazzle of gold. This heady sense of escape filled her being to the exclusion of her fear of being lost in the desert. She had a leather water-bottle strapped to her saddle, and these desert-bred horses were curiously intelligent. There was every hope that Beauty would take her straight to an oasis, where she might find an encampment of Persians who would help her. She could speak their language quite adequately, and was wearing rings and a gemmed wristwatch worth quite a bit, with which she could make payment for assistance out of reach of the *khan*.

She wouldn't mention him! She would merely say that

she was lost and required escort to the nearest township.

Her confidence billowed like her windswept cloak . . . and then came sudden and shocking deflation as Beauty, in his wild free motion, stumbled upon one of the sandstone rocks half buried in the sand. He had crashed headlong almost before Grace realized what had happened and with a scream on her lips she kicked free of the stirrups and felt herself flying out of the saddle as Beauty rolled, whinnying loud with pain, but away from her thanks to her instant action in freeing her legs and feet before the big animal could crush them beneath his agonized weight.

Grace herself landed in the soft sand and lay shaken and breathless . . . it was her mount's distress which brought her to her feet, and still dizzied by her fall, she lurched to Beauty's side and flung a hand over her mouth when she saw how he was rolling his eyes and baring his huge teeth in agony. She knew at once that he had snapped a foreleg, and her pity for him mingled with her fear of the *khan's* anger. She knew how much he valued his horses, which he bred from the very finest stock and hand-reared until they were sleek, lovely, spirited colts. She sank on to her knees just out of reach of Beauty's helpless, kicking legs, and though the sun was pouring down she felt shivery, torn between her compassion for the horse she had grown so fond of, and an instinctive terror of the man who would now catch up with her.

There was no escape from him after all . . . the desert itself was like his devilish incubus, aiding him to trap her by planting that cruel stone, half jutting in the sand, in the path of her galloping horse. And there across the surface of the glaring yellow sand lay the trail of hoof marks leading to her.

The desert all around her felt like a trap, for she knew it would be sheer lunacy for her to set out on foot in the scorching sun of mid-afternoon. Added to which she could not have brought herself to abandon the horse.

When at last he ceased to thresh about, Grace unhooked the water-bottle, filled the cap with water and carefully

tipped it into Beauty's mouth. He gazed at her so patheti-
cally when she did this that the tears came blindingly in her
eyes, and he allowed her to stroke his sweating neck, with
the pain-stretched muscles like cords beneath her hand. He
had been so vital, so swift and proud, and now because of
her (yes, it was all her fault) he lay in the hot sun with a
broken leg, and there was nothing she could do but wait for
the *khan* to arrive and take charge of them both.

She dreaded his coming, for it was like waiting for a
threatening storm to descend upon her, and with a little
groan she flung her arms across Beauty's neck and lay there
utterly still in her white muslin head-wear and her long
scarlet cloak. It would have been a relief if she could have
wept, but all she could do was listen to the deep beating of
the life-vein beneath the wet, silky chestnut coat of her
horse, and hear in the stillness all about them a sort of menace.

Then suddenly with all her nervous instincts alert, she
raised her head and stared with frightened eyes across the
sands that were hazy with heat. She had sensed the group of
horsemen before she actually saw them, and her heart
seemed to turn over when they actually appeared out of the
haze, coming at a killing pace across the desert towards her,
their great cloaks billowing around them like immense
wings . . . she might have thought them angels of mercy had
she not known, in her every nerve, that they were men of the
Haklyt Rohim, led by a blue-cloaked figure on a raking grey
stallion.

The grey horse and its rider came headlong across the
smouldering surface of the sand, a vivid and frightening picture which burned itself into Grace's vision . . . like a figure
of vengeance intent on riding her down. She leapt to her feet
almost unaware, as if about to take flight from Kharim
Khan, and as Beauty caught the sound of galloping hoofs he
began to thresh about again and to make those heartrending
horse sounds as he failed to rise from where he had fallen.

Sand whirled under the thundering hoofs of the grey stallion and he was brought to a prancing halt quite close to

where Grace was standing. The blue cloak flung out about the tall figure of the *khan* as he leapt from the saddle and stood there a moment just scowling at her. Never had she seen his brows so black, nor his eyes so dangerously green. 'You reckless little fool,' he said cuttingly. 'You have wilfully damaged a fine horse, so I see! Are you proud of yourself?'

Grace just stood there as if rooted to the sands; she couldn't move or speak as a sort of paralysis of fear took hold of her. His eyes were glittering with his anger and his features were every bit as cruel as she had imagined they could be. He took a step towards her and still she couldn't move . . . and then she found her voice and cried out as he thrust her to one side so that she stumbled on her nerveless legs and fell to the sands.

Without even a glance at her the *khan* approached the fallen horse and gentled him with a mere touch of those lean brown hands. Then he knelt and carefully examined the leg, and Grace winced and bit her ashen lips as she heard a curse fall from the grim lips of the *khan*. That doom-bell seemed to peal louder in her brain, and she crouched where she had fallen, like a small girl dreading the blow that was inevitable because she had caused an unforgivable mishap.

The *khan*'s men had galloped to the scene and one of them dismounted. Through weary, heat-bleared eyes Grace saw that the man was Davoud Sayed, striding in boots of pomegranate-red to where the *khan* offered what comfort he could to a horse which had fallen and broken a leg in the middle of the desert. A shudder swept all through Grace as she caught the mutter of words that passed between the two men, then Davoud came to her and bending over her touched her on the shoulder.

'Come, *lella*,' he said. 'We will ride a little way off, for the horse is to be destroyed.'

'Oh no!' Shock and torment released her limbs from their paralysis and she scrambled to her feet and ran to the *khan*, who had a hand at the revolver in his belt. 'No!' She flung herself at him. 'You can't do it, Kharim! I won't let you! It's a clean break and the leg can be mended — *you* know that. You're just going to shoot him to punish me—'

'Don't be more of a little fool than you have been already!' He caught her wrist in such a punishing grip that she went as white as a sheet and cried out with pain. 'We have no means of getting the horse to the encampment, where I might attend to him. He is suffering from pain and the heat, and if you won't go with Davoud, then stay!'

With these words he released her wrist from his grip, and a moment later the revolver was fired and poor Beauty lay still and out of his misery.

The tears rolled unaware down Grace's cheeks, and she was apathetic when the *khan* led her away from the spot where the chestnut horse lay so lifeless. A sob shook her, and there seemed nothing left to care about as the strong and ruthless hands swung her to the saddle of the grey stallion, and the deep voice curtly ordered her to take hold of the front of the saddle.

She did so, but couldn't drag her gaze from the still and silent figure of Beauty; he had been so full of mettlesome power, and Kharim Khan had deprived him of all that power just as she had planned to deprive the man of his. A shudder swept all through her as the *khan* swung into the saddle behind her, reached his strong arms around her and took the reins of his stallion. Immediately the grey started to jib, tossing its handsome head and long dark mane. The *khan* snapped out some words in Persian and at once the stallion broke into the long, loping gallop that ate up the miles of sand so that Grace's dead mount was soon left behind them.

She clung in a kind of daze to the saddle, and had just enough will-power left to sit straight and avoid physical contact with the man behind her. But her mind refused to be free of him. He crowded it with images, and the most vivid was the hard bronze set of his features when he had flung her into the saddle of his horse as if he would now like to throw her out of his life.

Oh, why did he keep her with him when she caused him nothing but trouble? Why didn't he let her go? What perverse streak of devilment drove him to endure a woman who had shown him again and again that she hated the position he had thrust upon her – that of a woman of caprice; a creature of passing pleasure; his makeshift companion. The Haklyt Rohim were not to know that pleasure was the last thing he got from her, but she supposed wearily that it was because they believed him to be her lover that he kept her with him, and came chasing after her in the full heat of the sun.

He had his pride, she knew that. No one was going to say that a woman ever got the better of him, one of the big, lordly, tribal *khans* of the Persian desert. She was his toy . . . until he finally wearied of the battle that went on in privacy between them.

How naïve she had been to believe that the Persian desert might hold peace for her . . . it held only conflict . . . only a constant sort of heartache for which there seemed no remedy. Strange was the fate which had thrown her into the power of Kharim Khan, for had her grandfather never taken her to Persia in the first place, there was every chance that she would never have visited the country. But once seen it was a place that played on the imagination and drew back to it those who had seen its sunsets and its lush, walled gardens.

She drew a sigh and her eyes were drawn to the sky that was flushing over as the time of the sunset drew near. In the desert time seemed eternal until one realized that the heat was fading to a blessed coolness as the hot day began to decline. A silent cry seemed to rise in her throat as she saw the long tongues of flame spreading from the golden globe of the sun, smouldering at the blueness of the sky and changing it to other colours; to violet streaked with apricot, to apple green blending into copper gold. Within this veil of glorious colour the sun seemed alive with a beautiful sort of agony, which very soon would be a burning death shrouded by black velvet night studded with a million stars.

The sands were waves of glowing gold sweeping to the edges of the creeping shadows. The dunes rose into crests of peachy colour spilling into pools of dark violet shadow, and a mysterious whispering wind came travelling across the sands, the voice of night declaring that the day was done and now it was the turn of the stars to make silver beauty where there had been a shimmering molten heat.

Grace could not deny the beauty, nor the drama of the desert ... a golden cage against whose invisible bars she bruised herself whenever she tried to escape. In her state of weariness she seemed to feel the hard tangibility of those bars ... until with a little jolt she half stirred awake to realize that it was the hardness of the *khan*'s arms that enclosed her.

In her weariness she had lost the will to sit upright and was now leaning against him and was unable to fight the pervading sense of ease which his physical strength imparted to her. She seemed to drift in a kind of limbo between childhood and adulthood, for in that limbo she could forget she was a woman with a man and could permit her achingly tired body to fall through a deep, velvety darkness into the oblivion of the sleep for which her racked emotions cried.

# CHAPTER NINE

It was sudden light against her eyelids that woke Grace from the deep slumber into which she had fallen. She blinked sleepily and was confused by her surroundings, until it came to her that she was inside a tent.

The *khan* and his men had arrived at the encampment while she slept, and she had been carried inside. Carpets had been slung down, and she had been laid upon a divan, but apart from the lamp which hung from the central beam of the tent it was sparsely furnished, as if not long erected.

When she sat up and looked around she saw the great blue cloak flung across the end of the divan, and her heart gave such a violent thump that a small cry escaped her. Now she remembered everything. The Haklyt Rohim had arrived at the foothills of Mahnaz; they had reached their destination and here they would erect their tents and let their animals roam the hills.

This was their summer home, and tonight they would celebrate their arrival with the marriage of the *khan*'s manservant to Shalena. As it all rushed back into Grace's mind, she pressed her hands to her eyes and realized how close she had come to spoiling for Shalena the happiness of her wedding. Grace knew in her very bones that the *khan* would have searched for her all night, until he found her again . . . not from love, or even the desire still unquenched, but from the sheer driving devilment of having her within his power. It was for him to decide when she no longer amused him. For him to grant lordly permission for her to leave.

She pressed her fingertips against her eyes and prayed for some semblance of composure when he arrived to find out if she had awoken from the sleep which had overcome her in his arms, out there in the dark desert, upon the shared saddle of his black-maned grey stallion. In retrospect it had been the strangest experience of her life; a kind of surrender to his arms, like a child, almost, trusting herself to him in the absolute helplessness of a body fatigued by his ruthless desert and the way it killed those who stood between them. She had let her head rest against him ... had pillowed her cheek against the blue cloak that when worn by him had a way of intensifying his look of bold authority and splendid command of his tall, lithe, erect body. The great blue folds swung from his wide shoulder and wrapped themselves with a grace entirely masculine about his hard, strong frame. So vivid was his personality, blending a certain lawless air with a total dedication to his people, that Grace could almost feel him in the tent with her. She flung up her head ... and there he was, standing just inside the flap, having approached in his soundless way and having entered while her hands were pressed to her eyes.

'You look as startled as if a serpent had slithered in,' he drawled. 'Are you feeling more rested? You were still deeply asleep when I carried you in here an hour ago. Slumbrous as a child, and yet a woman, with a face pale as a white lily, with deep shadows under your eyes. Are the shadows gone?' He took a stride across the carpets and suddenly he was leaning over her and looking keenly at her upraised face. 'You blame me for what happened to your horse, but if you had not galloped off in the first place – *mon enfant*, don't you begin to realize that life in the desert will be so much easier for you if you cease to be the little rebel? Why not give in? Why keep fighting and hurting yourself? Is it mere British courage and obstinacy, eh? Well, you have proved those, so now be sensible before something happens that will really harm you.'

'What, is there no harm in being with you?' She clutched at scorn in defence against his tall nearness, more disconcerting right now than it had ever been before. She couldn't forget that she had slept in his arms. She couldn't dismiss a mental picture of herself, helplessly asleep, her head nestling against the blue cloth covering his hard chest. She was ashamed of her own weak surrender to his strength.

'Shall I tell you, *mon ange*, exactly the sort of harm that could well come to you when you take it into your foolish head to ride off as you did today?' As he spoke he narrowed his eyes to a menacing green, and he took from a pocket of his trousers the slim leather case that held his cheroots. He extracted one, and lowering the lamp he bent his head to the open flame and ignited the end of the cheroot. As he straightened up the lamplight was upon his face and his features had that look of chiselled bronze, played over by the strong smoke stealing from his taut nostrils.

He stared down at Grace, his eyes glinting through the heavy blackness of his lashes. 'For your own good I am going to tell you what happened to a girl of the Haklyt Rohim only a couple of years ago. She was the young daughter of one of my best men, a girl of sixteen and very comely. There had been a rainfall, after which she wandered off to pick flowers from a nearby *wadi*. The hours passed and she failed to return to her father's tent. A search was organized and she was found a few days later. Some men — we believe them to have been soldiers — had presumably seen her in the *wadi* and they had carried her off with them to a small oasis, where we found her young body flung down a well. Stripped, ravished, dead as the flowers she had gone in search of. The shock and distress were so terrible for her father, for she was all the family that he had, that he took poison distilled from the oleander, and we buried them together in the desert.'

He paused there and flung ash from his cheroot. 'What a wedding gift for Achmed and Shalena if my men and I had found your body in the well of an oasis! So think of that, my lady, the next time you take it into your head to ride off alone, for in the desert the devil you know is truly preferable to the devil you don't know.'

His story of the murdered girl and her father had seemed to chill the blood in Grace's veins, for each word had fallen from lips set in such cruel lines. She felt quite sure that if the *khan* and his men had found the abductors of the girl, they would have suffered appallingly. The desert did not breed gentleness ... it bred hardihood and passion and a certain barbarism. All of these qualities were stamped on the features of Kharim Khan; bred into his bones, warm and fierce like a dark wine flowing in his veins. She could not condone the streak of barbarism in his nature, yet at the same time she could understand his deep anger regarding the girl, and his motive in telling the story to her.

'I'm sorry,' she said. 'I — I understand now why you took the trouble to come after me.'

'I'm glad of it.' A note of irony rang in his voice. 'Bath water is being brought to you, and I wish you to prepare yourself for the wedding. Your suitcases have been unpacked so you can select àn attractive dress to wear. And wear this, also!' An object landed in her lap as he turned away from her. 'Don't imagine I am rewarding you for a hot chase and a certain anxiety. I am insisting that you look at your best, for this marriage marks an important occasion for the Haklyt Rohim. They have arrived at *yilak*, our summer pasturage and, thanks to Allah, if not to a rather headstrong British girl, we have arrived without mishap to any member of the tribe. You will be ready in an hour, for this ceremony which will take place beneath the stars.'

He left the tent as he spoke, the flap falling into place behind him, leaving an intense silence and a sort of vacuum, in which Grace stared at the incredibly lovely thing he had flung so casually into her lap. This was no savage pendant such as he had given her the other day, but a lotus-flowered *chand bina* for her forehead. The lotus petals were made up of sky-blue enamel tipped with gold, and the band terminated in tiny ivory doves with spread wings.

Grace felt the beating of her heart as she studied the forehead band, and her thoughts winged back to her first visit to Persia, when in an oriental market Jonas had bought her a *chand bina* of pearls, which she had worn when she had attended with him the wedding at a Persian city house. If she had doubted before that Kharim Khan had first seen her at that wedding, had looked, admired, and left well alone, she no longer doubted as she let her fingers stray over the ivory doves of the *chand bina* he had just ordered her to wear at Shalena's wedding. It seemed rather nerve-shattering that he should wish to see her almost as she had looked when still a girl, unmarried, not yet widowed, nor yet his reluctant captive of the desert.

An hour, he had said. In one hour he expected her to be ready, and recalling the stern set of his mouth and chin, Grace jumped to her feet and hastened into the interior section of the tent. There she found a big brass ablution bowl steaming with water, her suitcases upon a stool, and blessedly no one to wait upon her. She didn't want company right now, and welcomed the fact that most of the women would be fussing around the bride, helping to dress her in her elaborate wedding costume, and applying the wedding henna to her hands, her feet, and parts of her face. It was all a ritual with a certain mystery attached to it; each henna pattern had its marital significance, each piece of jewellery, and each veil played a part in the joining together of Achmed and his virgin bride.

Grace knew that these people venerated a girl of purity as if she were a goddess, and like a pagan goddess she would be adorned from her ankles tinkling with little bells to her intricate coiffure, crowned by a tiara of pearls. She would speak only a few words, and for the most part would be silent and adored, until at the stroke of midnight she would be carried to her bridegroom's tent.

Grace stood in the ablution bowl and soaped her pale, slim body with the palm-oil soap that was delicately perfumed and deliciously soothing to her skin, which had been exposed to the heat and hardship of desert travel for the past ten days. She knelt to rinse off the soap, and her arms were half raised, her hair was pinned above her neck, and she had somehow the look of an innocent sybarite, caught unaware at her bath, as all at once the curtain was swept aside and there was a gleam of ox-blood boots as the *khan* stepped into the alcove.

Instantly Grace froze, was held immobile, glistening with water there in the brass bowl as the *khan* stepped casually past her and picked up a small leather case, latched with a silver clasp, which lay on the mirror-chest near where she bathed.

'My razor and shaving-soap,' he drawled. 'You will excuse the interruption, but I, too, wish to look my best tonight. *Au 'voir, ma petite*. I am in no doubt that you will look charming.'

With these words, spoken with so much meaning, he was gone again, and Grace felt as if she blushed all over her body. God, what a devil he was! No woman, no matter how hard she tried, or how often she hoped, would ever subdue or tame him. He had known she was taking her bath, yet without a by-your-leave, a polite cough, or a request that she hand him his shaving-kit, he had entered the alcove as if there was such casual intimacy between them that he had every right to see her without a stitch upon her body.

She snatched one of the big bath-towels and hugged it around her. It was humiliating to be so without the privacy of her own bathroom, her own bedroom, her own way of life. She was forced to share a tent with a man who took upon himself more privileges than her husband had taken. Not even Tony would have strolled into her bathroom as this man had done, and the arrogant devil had not even had the grace to turn his eyes away! Not wasting another second, she rubbed herself dry, dashed cologne over her skin, and scrambled into her lingerie. Her dress was laid out on the ottoman in the other room and she peered through the curtain before venturing into the bedroom, just in case he was there. She gave a sigh of relief when she saw that the room was empty, and picking up her dress she slipped it down over her head and fastened the amber sash that was the only highlight of the ivory-silk dress.

Still burning a little from the *khan*'s invasion of her privacy, Grace decided that an aloof hairstyle was called for, something that would make her feel haughty and cool when next they met. One thing about wearing the muslin turban while she rode in the desert was that it saved her hair from getting sunburned and full of sand grains, and after brushing her tresses she arranged them into a shining knot *à la greque*, and then she added the forehead band of glowing blue, gold and ivory, and had to admit to herself that the effect was graceful, allied to her softly flowing dress. Renaissance, she thought. Almost as if she had stepped out of the canvas of an Ingres painting. She wasn't being vain, but coolly objective about herself. Tonight she needed to look untouchable, and what was more so than an aloof picture in a frame?

Taking up her scarlet cloak, she walked into the lounging area of the tent. It was empty but for a tang of cheroot smoke, a reminder that he had been here and would shortly reappear. Grace drew her cloak closer about her, for to think of him was to feel his presence; his vitality lingered in the air of a room as the tangy smoke did. She ran a hand up the smooth nape of her neck, for much as she tried she couldn't dismiss the fact that Kharim Khan was no ordinary man. He was absolute master of his tribe; the great-grandson of the Persian war-lord Khan Rahi, and he knew it! He merely shrugged from his broad shoulders his crime of abduction, which for him followed naturally on having seen her and desired her. He had taken her away with him as he would a pomegranate from a tree . . . his only virtue lay in restraining himself from tasting his stolen fruit.

He was extraordinary, and Grace knew it! Bold, wilful, mocking, and yet with a subtle sense of humour she had not found in Jonas, nor in Tony. She had obeyed Jonas out of a sense of duty and had never really fought with him, or laughed with him. She had fought with Tony, but always with a sense of contempt rather than a feeling of wild rebellion culminating in a sense of shock each time she was mastered by the *khan*, and looked at with twin devils glinting in his jade-green eyes . . . the devil of danger, and the devil of amused indulgence.

As Grace stood awaiting him, she wondered just how far his leash would stretch with regard to her. What were his plans now they had reached Mahnaz and were at the foot of the hills that were dominated by his palace?

Then she tautened where she stood, her nerves reacting

155

with a primitive awareness of his approach. The flap of the tent was swept to one side and there was a rustle of a great cloak as he stepped inside and the tall shadow of him was flung by the lamp up the wall of the tent. At once, instinctively, they faced each other like creatures of a different species, tense with suspicion and unrest, and a certain curiosity.

Grace saw that beneath his dark-blue cloak with a silver edging he wore a kaftan that shimmered with peacock hues, and dark-blue pants swathed into fine leather boots. His headdress, also of blue, was bound with an *agal* of gold, and never had Grace seen him clad so splendidly, so that all that was foreign in him was brought out vividly, to form an image both commanding and picturesque.

He was, at one and the same time, the most terrifying man she had ever seen, and the most physically resplendent. Sleekly muscled under his princely robes, with a firm brown skin pelting his strong body, with eyes that could smoulder with a gem-like quality, and glitter with a ruthless, unpredictable light.

*Un homme de bon air*, she thought. A prince in his own right, and on display tonight, for as the *agha* of the Haklyt Rohim, the master of them all, he gave away the bride to Achmed.

'Remove your cloak for a moment,' he ordered. 'Let me see you.'

For once she made no attempt to disobey him and allowed the folds of her scarlet cloak to fall away from her bare arms and her slim body clad in the classically simple dress of ivory-white silk. His eyes felt like green fire as they travelled over her, from her Grecian coiled hair, set off by the *chand bina*, down over her graceful figure to her satin slippers.

'You look not unlike a bride yourself,' he drawled. 'Shall we make a double ceremony of tonight's wedding?'

'Don't say such things!' she exclaimed. 'It's irreverent, apart from being your idea of a joke!'

'It could well be *mon ange*, that I am not joking.' Then

156

his teeth gleamed whitely as she drew back from him and clasped the red cloak around her, as if seeking some sort of protection from him. '*Je suis désolé, ma petite fille*, I forget the disastrous experience of marriage which you have already endured. Naturally, I speak in jest! As if a lady of snow would ever dream of leaping into the furnaces of emotion a man of my race is capable of feeling. You would melt right away, eh? Be lost to your own self ... the ultimate of love, so they say. The supremest sacrifice a woman can make.'

'And what of a man?' As the question sprang from her lips, she could feel her fingers crushing the heavy silk of her cloak. She thought how superbly, arrogantly sure he was of himself. Love for him was just a matter of the senses; a pleasure to be snatched, then tossed as casually to one side as he would toss the cloak in which he rode, and wrapped himself against the night winds of the desert. Love was rarely as important to a man as it was to a woman; least of all to a man who had the guidance and the leadership of his people to put before anything personal in his life.

Love for him was passion; there in his lips lay the savagery and the sensuality which had led him to snatch her for his pleasure ... what held him back was the fact of her innocence. While she remained in the state of chastity she was a holy thing to a Persian male, untouchable and inviolate, and as the irony of the situation struck at Grace, she flung back her head and gave a laugh.

'Marriage would be so easy for you, would it not, Kharim Khan? For divorce would also be easy. All you would need to say are the traditional words, "Begone! Once, twice, thrice, I repudiate thee!" In that way you would have the best of both worlds, with none of the condemnation of your Persian gods.'

'How well you presume to know me.' His jade eyes were rampant with mockery. 'How well taught you are in judging all men alike.'

'Aren't they alike?' she flung at him. 'Out to suit themselves, and to hell with a woman's feelings. What really changes in this life? The women who delude themselves about equality are the biggest fools of all. Until the moon falls out of the sky they will bear the children and endure the emotional burdens . . . the male of the species will always have more freedom.'

'You are wishing you were a boy? He quirked an eyebrow as once again he let his eyes dwell upon her hair, her face, her cloak-wrapped figure. 'In truth you would not be here if such were the case, but just think, *mon ange*, of all you would have missed! The freedom of the desert, though you call it a prison. And the freedom – though you deny it – to speak with me as you have never spoken with a man in your life. The gates of your mind have been flung open, even if the gates of your heart remain closed. Come!' He gestured at the tent flap and held it open. 'Let us go to the wedding!'

Grace moved towards him and each step intensified his dark splendour, his tallness, and the devils agleam in his eyes. Her cloak brushed against him and her nostrils tensed to the aroma of sandalwood that clung to him, as if his kaftan and cloak had been taken from one of those Persian chests that were lined with the aromatic wood. She heard him laugh softly as she passed him. 'You foolish child,' he mocked. 'Be thankful that you are a girl, for if you weren't and you spoke with such a lack of deference to a *khan*, you would be lucky not to receive seven strokes of the whip.'

'Really?' she said, feeling a return of confidence as she stepped into the starlight that was flooding the desert sands. 'What due deference should I show to my lord Kharim Khan?'

'A respectful kiss on the shoulder, if you were male. But as you are a female, there are other places on my person that would be more, far more appreciative of your kisses.'

'I am sure, my lord, that my kisses would be too cool for you.' And with a cool demureness she gazed up at the immensity of the sky, studded by the many enormous Eastern stars. Each one seemed to burn with bright points of fire that blended to create an effect of a sky aflame with silver. The scene was awesome and beautiful beyond words, and across the aeons of space stole the rustling sound of sand grains settling down after the intense heat of the day, added to which, tonight, was the soft creaking of the palm trees as the wind sighed through their crowns. Her eyes took in the savage, thrusting grace of the palm trees that grew abundantly here at Mahnaz, where the winds were softer and where water ran under the ground. She knew that high among the pendant leaves were honey-coloured bunches of dates, and she felt sure that they added to the honey scent pervading the night, in which mingled the tang of the camp fires on to which had been thrown aromatic twigs of wild mint and tamarisk.

It was an exciting perfume, stealing from the fires that flickered among the velvety sand-dunes, and Grace would have been less than human if she had not felt a responsive excitement.

The *khan* must have felt it also, for all at once he quoted Kipling in his deep foreign voice, intensifying the meaning of the words. ' "Scents are surer than sounds or sights to make your heartstrings crack." Don't you agree, my lady?'

'Yes – the air tonight is glorious.' Her eyes were burnished by the stars as she glanced at him and saw that his face had a strong, pagan beauty by the silvery light of the stars. The long brows merged like thick dark silk above his flashing eyes, and his nose had a dominant distinction above the bold curving of his lips and the deep clefting of his firm chin. He was as noble and savagely graceful as the tall palm trees ... and Grace was confused by this nobility which seemed at odds with his capricious behaviour with regard to her.

Right now she had to go with him among his people, and she had to submit to their belief that she was his *kadin*. Because they were lusty, earthy desert people they would not believe anything else of the woman who shared the blue tent with their *khan*. They couldn't know, as he did, that she had never been a real wife to Tony and was therefore as bodily innocent as the girl Shalena.

The soft night breezes could not cool her cheeks as she felt the dark Persian eyes appraising her, for with a flick of his hand the *khan* had removed her cloak and she stood there in the firelight, as slim and pale as a segment of the starlight itself, the flames leaping high to reflect in the shining blue and gold of the band holding her hair. She knew that to most of these people her fair looks were alien and her mode of dress rather strange, but if to their *khan* she was his 'pearl of joy' then they were more than ready to accept her as one of them.

She was bowed to and greeted as she stood there beside him, but reciprocal words seemed locked in her throat, and she gave a nervous start as the *khan* suddenly bent his head to hers and murmured in her ear: 'Relax, *ma chérie*. No sad eyes must rest upon the bride or her felicity will not be complete. Is it so impossible for you to enjoy yourself with me, among my sons and daughters? As their *khan* I am their godfather, though I don't doubt that you regard me as their devil's disciple.'

'No—' The word broke from her . . . no, it wasn't true that she thought him less of a leader, because he acted the pirate with her. And then she was able to smile as Shalena suddenly appeared from her mother's tent, wrapped in the long *chaddur* of shimmering gold net, the veil that concealed as if by magic the former self of the bride, now to become a different person, to face a fortunate fate, or an unhappy one. No one could know but the gods, and so she was covered from head to toe in the long veil, beneath which she would be wearing trousers of shimmering silk, a many-coloured shift, and a jacket of embroidered velvet. There would be patterns of wedding henna on her forehead, the palms of her hands and the soles of her feet, to bring her joy and love.

Attractive goods, bundled in a beguiling wrapper, thought Grace. As Rebecca, upon marrying Isaac, 'Took the veil and covered herself.'

The *khan* left Grace's side as the bride appeared and discarding his own cloak, which Davoud Sayed accepted, he stepped forward and taking the hand of the bride he led her to where Achmed stood in the firelight with the robed patriarch who would marry them. The firelight gleamed on the gold binding of the *Qur'an* in the gnarled hands of the tribal priest, who would conduct the marriage verbally though it would not be registered. It was sufficient for these people that the oaths were taken on the Koran, and that the stars — the many eyes of Allah — looked down upon the ceremony.

As in a dream Grace watched it all, was part of it without being of these people; of their blood, their heritage, their primitive loyalties and passions.

The other day, with childlike eagerness Shalena had shown Grace the painted box which Achmed had given her, in which lay the traditional gifts of a fiancé. The sweet loaves of sugar and the sack of tea. The beautiful silk shawl, the ring set with diamonds, and a pair of golden earhoops.

Now, as the age-old *Qur'an* words joined them in marriage, the bridegroom lifted the *chaddur* and sweetened Shalena's lips with sugar, and she in turn sweetened his. The veil fell to her shoulders and there in her ears were the golden hoops, placed there by a friend who was the mother of children. On her fine-boned, hennaed hand was the diamond ring, and on her head was a circlet of pearls, handed down from her mother.

The words of the old priest echoed in the firelight. 'Now, sayeth Allah, be as one like heaven, sky and earth. Now go forth, in the hands of fate and fortune. Allah be with you both!'

They were married, and each pair of lips was pressed to the *Qur'an*, for the bridal kisses would be exchanged in private. The *khan*, towering above them in his kaftan of shifting dark colours, joined their hands and murmured his own traditional words of good fortune. Then he left them standing shyly there, while his gift to the bride and groom were brought forward. His gift to Shalena was a lovely creamcoated pony wearing turquoise harness, and with forelegs hennaed for the occasion. His gift to Achmed was a leather wallet of money, enough for the couple to build a house, if they so wished, or to buy a flock of the fat-tailed sheep favoured by the Haklyt Rohim.

As Grace stood apart and watched the colour and drama of this wedding by starlight, it struck her again as rather awesome that so young a man should be in command of so many people, from distinguished tribal patriarchs to slim young beauties and babes in arms.

The wailing notes of the Persian violin began to play, and a chair was brought from one of the tents for the bride, who would now sit in 'state' while relatives and friends came to wish her happiness. For the time being the bridegroom disappeared among a group of male friends, to enjoy with them the wedding feast of roast partridge and pheasant, not to mention the huge mounds of lamb and chicken *pilaff*. Intoxicating wine would not be served, for this was a desert wedding and the Haklyt Rohim were strictly Moslem. Instead there was plenty of tea and coffee, and cordials made from the wild fruits, including the pomegranate.

Grace, battling with a certain shyness because she was so much the stranger at the wedding, approached the chair in which Shalena sat like a lovely idol. The long, cobweb-fine veil was now loose about her figure, so that the guests might admire her wedding garments and the circlet of pearls crowning the intricate weaving of her shining dark hair. Although her young face was suitably grave for the occasion, Grace saw at once the deep glow to the immense brown eyes; the well of love bubbling there for Achmed. It didn't matter to Shalena that he was older than she, nor as handsome as some of the other young bloods of the Haklyt Rohim. He was a man of warm heart, and a man of position, for he attended personally on the *khan*. He was the husband Shalena desired, and not a single cloud marred this wedding for the Persian girl.

How different from her own wedding to Tony, thought Grace. But none of the regret showed in her smile as she leaned forward to kiss Shalena's cheek and to murmur that the ceremony had been beautiful. As she spoke she pressed into Shalena's hand the gift of a pair of diamond bracelets; they were pretty and valuable and would add to the Persian girl's status among the women of the camp. 'With all my best wishes, Shalena. You make a perfectly lovely bride.'

'*Lella*, you are so kind!'

'Am I, I wonder?' With a sudden quiver to her lips Grace withdrew from the cluster of guests around the bride, and all at once, hands gripping the flowing skirt of her dress, she began to make for the palm trees where there were aisles of shadow where she might walk for a while with her restless thoughts.

But this wasn't to be; she had gone but a few yards when the deep voice of the *khan* arrested her and she spun round to face him, the high flames of the fires reflected in her pensive eyes. 'What are you doing? Attempting to run away again? If this goes on I shall have to keep you on a lead!' He reached out and the sash of her dress was caught between his fingers like the fluttering wing of a moth. 'Come, you will eat supper with me. I am sure you are hungry after those hours in the desert.'

It was useless to argue with him, for he had hold of her and his people were watching them. She went with him to where a large, handwoven rug of many colours was laid on the sands. He gestured her to sit down and he sprawled beside her, and almost at once food was brought to them. Grace caught a wicked gleam of white teeth as the *khan* picked up a leg of partridge with his fingers.

'If you don't eat, then the bride's family will assume that you aren't pleased with the food,' he said. 'Eat, child! Forget yesterday, don't think about tomorrow and just live for to-night.'

'I can quite understand that philosophy to be yours, but I am not a child of the stars,' she rejoined. 'It isn't quite so easy for me to throw off the cloak of convention.'

'So I have noticed, but force yourself, if only for the sake of that young girl who has just become a bride and who must sit there like a pretty figure of wax while the aroma of all which is far more taxing than yours. Think if that were you sitting there!' His eyes mocked her as his teeth tore at the hot succulent bird. 'Having to look as composed and cool as the acacia flower while everyone stares at you except for your bridegroom, whose role is to ignore you until the time arrives for him to – possess you. It would not do for the bridegroom to be too eager. He has to teach his bride that he is still his own master, and the Persian girl loves this. She wouldn't care to be married to a man she could mould as if he were the bread-dough for her oven. There is a saying that Allah made a man upright so that he could look at the stars, and that he made a woman upright so she could look at the man.'

'Well, as I'm not a Persian girl,' said Grace, reaching for a wing of bird, 'I don't have to take such nonsense seriously. No man is worth a crick in the neck as far as I'm concerned. The sheer masculine gall of such a remark would be laughable if it weren't insulting.'

'I agree,' he said, surprising her. 'Men aren't gods but very fallible human beings. Nor are women angels, even those who look as if they might be.'

'*Touchée*,' she said, as his green eyes flickered over her. 'You look like – a sprawled leopard satisfying your hunger.'

'I am glad to see that you are satisfying yours. You must try some of the *pilaff*, and of course some pomegranate cordial.'

It looked and tasted rather like pink champagne, while Grace had to admit to herself that never had food tasted so good, flavoured as it was by the aromatic smoke of the fires and the spices which had been added. She had thought that food would choke her after the traumatic events of the day, but instead she was amazed by how hungrily she ate *pilaff*, and the immense slice of pink-fleshed watermelon which the *khan* cut for her from one of the big green-skinned fruits. It cleaned her palate and cooled her throat of the tangy spices.

She looked around her and saw that she and the *khan* seemed to be islanded on the colourful rug, for everyone else seemed to be a member of a large group of relatives. A haze of smoke overhung their feasting and their laughter, and for the first time Grace actively realized that Kharim Khan, being the man in command, was also a rather lonely man. If he had a family then they probably lived at the palace, but somehow he never struck Grace as a family man. From what she had gathered from Davoud Sayed the *khan* had taken on the cloak of authority at a fairly young age, when his mother had died. He might not have found time just yet to found a family of his own .. there was every probability that he was betrothed to a girl who was still considered too immature to become his wife. Persian betrothals took place very often when a girl was still in the nursery, and by tradition, by his very heritage, he could only marry a girl from another clan as powerful as his own. A distant cousin, perhaps.

As sudden curiosity stirred through Grace she looked at him and saw that his features were etched forcibly by the firelight, something almost brooding about the set of his lips. A girl had started to dance in the circle of the fires, bare-footed but wearing bright petticoats and a full-sleeved embroidered blouse. She danced to the music of a zither and the low throbbing of drums. She swayed with the primitive grace of a palm-branch, whirled her shapely body and pounded the sand with her brown feet. And all the time her burning dark eyes, the almond-shape of them intensified by the outlines of kohl, were fixed upon the *khan*. She was dancing for him, the beaded rings in her ears gleaming against her long jetty hair, washed in indigo to bring out the dark blue lights, while the silver amulets about her ankles made a barbaric music of their own. She was no doe-eyed, pretty creature such as Shalena, but an agile gipsy of a girl, her skin the colour of dark honey, and her admiration of the *khan* on full display for everyone to see.

She ignored Grace as if she were not there, twirling her skirts and revealing her long and shapely legs. Closer, closer, like a leopardess in search of a mate ... and then as the drumbeats quickened, as the dancer seemed about to fling herself at the *khan*, he flung coins at her feet, and as a ripple of masculine laughter rang in the shadows beyond the firelight, Grace realized that Kharim Khan had paid the girl for her dancing and was uninterested in the offer she was making of her person.

Then, for the first time, the dancer looked directly at Grace, with eyes that seemed to rip off her dress. Then, bending down in supple time to the music, the girl snatched up one of the coins and flung it right at Grace. It was a golden Persian coin and it stung Grace's bare arm as it hit against her. Immediately the *khan* tensed and would have sprung to his feet if Grace hadn't caught at his arm. 'No!' she said. 'Please!'

His eyes flashed to her face and they were glittering with a leopard-green anger. 'You realize—?'

'Yes.' Grace spoke in a low voice. 'Please forget it – don't spoil Shalena's wedding.'

'Very well.' He glanced down at her fingers gripping the sleeve of his kaftan; pale, fine-boned, with a desperate tenseness to the knuckles. 'I can see that you understand what has been implied. I am sorry—'

'It's a little late for being sorry.' Grace released his sleeve, and saw that the dark dancer had slipped away, gone with the rest of her coins, and that a mounting excitement seemed to surround the bride. Was it almost midnight? Was it almost time for Shalena to go to her bridegroom's tent?

As she watched, Achmed appeared with his friends. In their flowing robes they looked not unlike a band of marauders about to carry off the girl to her ravishment rather than her bridal bed. A glance at Shalena confirmed this impression, for the big dark eyes were now looking huge and apprehensive. A strange little shiver ran through Grace, for there was a primitive element here which was both terrifying and curiously fascinating. She couldn't take her eyes from the carrying off of Shalena to her husband's tent, the entrance of which was hung with small bells and amulets to ensure that their felicity was not disturbed by the smallest imp of evil. The amulets would protect, and the bells would tinkle if anything came to their door on this their wedding night.

The wedding drums were pounded as the flaps of the tent admitted bride and groom ... and in that moment, as the lamplight glimmered in the interior of the tent, Grace saw Shalena suddenly tighten her arms about Achmed's neck. Love for him had overcome her moment of terror, as love was meant to do.

Then Grace almost jumped out of her skin as a hand touched her arm. She turned sharply and found the *khan* towering above her. 'You are swaying on your feet with tiredness,' he said. 'Come to bed.'

At his words, at his touch, at his look of barbaric dominance as he stood there in the garments that made him look so Persian, Grace started back from him with her every nerve and sinew on the defensive. At once his face hardened as his green eyes read her thoughts in her blue eyes.

'What is the matter now?' he mocked. 'Do you imagine I am affected by the general air of nuptial bliss and am about to carry you to my tent?'

And for once Grace was lost for words; they seemed locked in her throat, and her body seemed gripped by a strange and helpless feeling. It was like a dream ... she wanted to run, but she couldn't move; she wanted to beg him to leave her alone, but the words wouldn't come. Then all at once, with a muttered word that might have been an oath, the *khan* flung his arms about her body and gathered her up with easy, almost unrelenting strength. He held her so closely to him that she lost her breath and felt that her head was spinning as he carried her away from the crowd of guests, who had broken into a Persian love song and were swaying to the music and softly clapping their hands in time with it.

The stars had grown so lustrous above the palm trees that Grace felt blinded by them as she was carried to the blue tent. His shoulder knocked aside the flap and his footfalls were silenced by the rugs as she was borne into the sleeping apartment, swiftly, as if by a man whose emotions were rising up to dominate him. He reached the side of the ottoman, outlined in soft shadows by the single, low-burning lamp, and quite deliberately he stood at the bedside a moment, gazing with dangerous eyes at Grace's frightened face.

'Aren't you going to weep and plead for my mercy?' he taunted. 'Come, *mon ange*, don't rob me of the pleasure of those trickling tears down the lovely cheeks, the pummelling fists and the struggles. I'm a barbarian and I am only happy when I am slaking my low desert passions on a poor helpless woman. Do rouse yourself from your state of shock and let me feel I have a woman in my arms instead of a lump of marble.'

Grace stared back at him, and the most curious thing of all was that never had she felt less like crying. How sure were his arms, and how firm and brown his throat framed by the collar of his kaftan. The strands of gold were agleam against the folded blue of his turban, accentuating the dark majesty of his features.

How strong a face, and how unlike the spoiled, peevish, fair-skinned face of Tony. How stamped with an ancient breeding, an ingrained culture, an authority that had drawn fine lines beside his eyes.

He stared down at her for what seemed a thousand flashing seconds, and then quite suddenly he dropped her to the bed, a pale, silk-clad figure against the dark fur coverlet.

'You look like a pale Cleopatra,' he said, through his teeth, 'minus her Antony, and hating her Caesar!'

With these words he turned on his heel, but when he reached the *maille* of beads he stood there a moment, clenching them. 'Tomorrow at the Palace of the Pomegranate there will be a door for you to lock. I advise you to do so . . . until I can find the time to take you back to your own people.'

Then he was gone and only the swish and rattle of the beads remained to be heard. Grace lay staring at the emptiness of the room, and the beads as they moved back and forth seemed like stones of hail hitting against her heart. Never had she felt such a strange sensation, and as if to protect herself against this feeling, she turned over and buried herself in the fur of the ottoman bed.

# CHAPTER TEN

BELOW stretched the beaten gold of the sands, but up here it was like being in the heart of the coolest and most glorious garden of Eden. That was truly how it seemed as they left behind them the hot desert and found themselves in the high hills of Mahnaz.

Mahnaz! Clothed with rich green grass that shimmered in the soft, refreshing air that blew upon it. Already, as early as dawn, the Haklyt Rohim shepherds had herded their heavy-tailed sheep up the slopes and the big woolly creatures were running about as if intoxicated, snuffing and gobbling the grass for all they were worth. Here at *yilak* they would drop their lambs, here where the grass was high and the air was balmy.

Mahnaz, the tribal headquarters, held each generation in the iron hand of the *khan*, the man born to take charge, if he were strong enough, and popular enough with the tribe. And Kharim Khan, they said, was a chip off the iron block that the Khan Rahi had been, a tall, eagle-nosed warrior who had made his tribe so powerful that they still could not be touched by the military without striking back as swiftly as a snake touched by a stick.

And here in the hills was built the tribal palace, and Grace could feel the quick beating of her heart as she and the *khan* rode along a mountain track that would bring them in sight of the place where she would stay, he said, until he found the time to take her back among her own people.

Her fingers tightened on the reins of the new mount he had given her, a supple, satin-coated black who flung up his head and jangled his bridle at her play on the reins. Was it truly possible that loud-mouthed, demanding, gossiping women like Mrs. Landon St. John were her own sort of people? Were men like Michael Thorpe the kind of men she liked? Good-natured, flirtatious polo-players and dancing partners ... men who seemed cut from thick cardboard in comparison to that hard, sunburned figure who rode at her side on his black-maned grey, the heavy folds of his blue cloak spread out against the muscular flanks of the stallion.

Grace felt a stab of emotion, shocking in its intensity, striking through her entire body from the nape of her neck down her spine to the very heels of her feet in the long, wine-coloured boots. For seconds on end the sensation was merciless and cruel, holding her fast in its grip and not letting go until her self-confession that the thought of leaving the *khan* was unbearable.

In some indefinable and bewitching way he had become loved instead of loathed, but for so long had Grace held her emotions in an ice-cool grip that her inner turmoil did not show itself when Kharim glanced at her and told her that very soon she would get her first glimpse of the Palace of the Pomegranate.

Her face against the pale swathing of her *shesh* had the cool and lovely privacy it always had; it didn't show at all that her inner feelings had been shattered like ice, for even as her heart was melting, her pride was defending her against him. He had desired her, and then been chilled by her icy indifference. Now he only marked time before letting her go.

His eyes slipped over her face, as if searching for some glimmer of interest, some small rift in her look of cool composure. As she felt him turning in the saddle to look at her, she hung on to her composure as if it were a lifeline thrown over a cliff from which she had half fallen. It meant everything to her that he shouldn't guess how she felt about him ... she felt sure he would be mockingly amused if he knew that the bird of desire had flown to her shoulder and had its talons in her heart.

'You should enjoy the palace, now you know that I am not going to make a prisoner of you.' A smile of irony flickered on his lips. 'It might make up a little for subjecting you to the rigours of my desert, which is somewhat different from the desert of the luxury traveller. You have, my lady, stood up remarkably well to the trek, for we made very few stops during the daytime. You are no wilting flower, are you? There is steel in that slender spine of yours, no doubt inherited from the rugged grandfather.'

'There is iron and fire in yours,' she rejoined, gazing straight ahead of her so there was no chance of him looking into her eyes ... the traitor eyes that might reveal her as a woman revealed to herself at long last. 'You are no doubt a very large chip off the Persian warlord who was your great-grandfather.'

She heard that soft ironic laugh of his, which seemed to play over her nerve-ends as never before, sending little quivers almost painful through her body; tiny arrows tipped with the fire that was melting swiftly the ice maiden he had called her.

'If I had charm and grace of manner I should no doubt be more popular with you, my lady, but if I had only those qualities my tribe would soon be uncontrollable. Out of the very love of my people I must be firm, ruthless, responsible for them, and in control of them. They are not city dwellers tamed to the hand; they are wild, bred of the Persian desert, part of its freedom, its cruelty, and its golden beauty. My people are like colts unbroken to the saddle, and so I have to be a sort of rogue stallion in order to lead them. They would not follow a milksop, *mon enfant*.'

*I know*, she wanted to cry out, but her lips were firmly compressed against the cry, and her chin had taken a tilt that looked like scorn and protected her against him.

'It is sad to be a realist, eh?' he murmured.

'Why sad?' she asked.

'Because the realist must see people as they are and not as images woven of his desires and his dreams. For some it is more than sad it is heartbreaking, but the heart can only truly break a few times in one's life and then it hardens and functions only to keep a man alive. *Assez*! We grow *très serieux*, and that is not the way for anyone to arrive home.'

Abruptly he cantered ahead of her to the end of the

mountain path, to where it suddenly branched away. There he brought his mount to a halt, reining in so that the stallion reared up and pawed the air, its rider outlined in his great cloak of blue against the mountains and the azure sky. As the stallion settled down, the *khan* sat there, gazing fixedly at what lay beyond that next bend.

Grace cantered up to join him, and the breath felt as if it stopped in her throat as she had her first glimpse of Kharim Khan's 'home'.

Beautiful and barbaric, it stood against the rocky, tree-clad slopes, a palace of marigold-stone, slumbering in the sun on its high plateau. Its Persian towers seemed made of gold, and its dome of lapis-lazuli. It was old, and yet as insubstantial as an image in a dream. Dark-winged hawks wheeled about its high towers, while a flutter of doves rose and fell about the fluted columns of its pavilion, like specks of silver in the air. Above upon the terraces were hanging cypress trees, and blazing against the stone, like balls of fire, were the blood-red pomegranates and those as golden as the sun itself.

Almost unaware, Grace had cantered with the *khan* nearer and nearer to the palace until they reached the tall gates and they swung open to welcome them.

While the *khan* spoke to members of his staff in the court-yard, men in dazzling white turbans and tunics and the tightly-swathed pants, Grace sat still in the saddle of her black horse and let her eyes feast on this, the private *kasba* of a powerful, wealthy, much adored and respected lord of the desert.

Lustrous jade-green tiling paved the pavilion, overlaid by oriental designs in various colours. Lizards gripped claws in the stonework of its columns, of a silvery fluted green. Poin-settias blazed in shafts of sunlight, immense billows of oleander, pink, scarlet and white, gave off a sharp scent to which the great bees flocked. There was a wall entangled with columbine, a great curtain of morning glory mantling the cloisters beneath the upper apartments of the palace, whose windows were enclosed in richly carved cages of cedarwood, through which the women of the household could look down into the pavilion without being seen.

Harem lattices, thought Grace, as she turned her head to watch the tumbling of water down over the tiled basins of a fountain. Her gaze climbed upwards to the marble balustrade of the highest terrace crowned by the burning blue dome.

She knew instinctively that the Palace of the Pomegranate had been built by the warlord whose blood ran in Kharim's veins. She had thought it a myth but knew it now to be a fact that men who lived hard, fierce and dangerous lives had to have something of beauty in their lives. A place of beauty, a retreat of pleasure and peace, where the flowers bloomed and the bees hummed, and small birds the colour of the turquoise flew on carved wings.

The place was magical, haunted, enticing. It seemed like a place of secret gardens, and summers of a boy's forgotten days of carefree youth. Too soon for Kharim Khan had duty called, to take him into the desert, away from the cool cloisters, the Persian blue tiles, the huge and shady fig trees, the shell-basins of the fountain, and the sweet taste of the pomegranate fruit.

Things she had not understood about Kharim's character were now made keener, up here in the clear air of Mahnaz, where everything grew in such profusion because the foliage and the flowers were kept moist by the mountain streams and not burned by the sun. She had surely found Sheba's garden at last, only to know that one day soon she would be turned out of it.

That she had fallen in love with Kharim could not alter anything. He had only wanted the strangeness of her, and could never love a woman not of his own heritage.

The bee-eaters flashed their wings in the shafts of sunlight, and Grace dragged her gaze from the flaming cypress trees and the clouds of white jasmine, tensing as Kharim came to the side of her horse and offered a hand so that she might dismount from the rather upright Persian saddle. Her own English saddle had been forgotten and left in the desert on the back of Beauty, after he had been shot. By now some nomads would have found it.

'Thank you.' On her feet beside Kharim she gave her spine a slight rub, for she had been in the saddle since early morning and it must now be close to noontime.

'Soon you will be able to soak for as long as you like in a real bath of water, overflowing and hot,' he said. 'But in the meantime – what do you think of the palace?'

'It's very beautiful,' she said, and quite deliberately she kept a note of restraint in her voice. 'It's wonderful to see so many exotic flowers after the barren gold of the desert. Everything must grow here, from the rose to the pumpkin vine.'

'Yes,' he agreed, looking round at the flower-hung pavilion. 'But wait until you see the various gardens. My grandmother was an ardent creator of gardens and she had seeds and roots flown from many parts of the world so that she could take advantage of the moisture-fed soil. She rarely left the palace, for the hot and stony desert did not appeal to her. Now come, I'll take you to your apartments. Your baggage won't arrive just yet, for the men are busy at present settling their flocks, but I have given instructions that cool clothing be provided for you. It will be a relief, eh, to discard the breeches and shirt? Bathe, eat, rest, then discover the gardens for yourself.'

'Thank you,' she said again, and she was being the polite guest to his courteous host, and was inwardly distracted that the sparks had died out of their sparring. She walked with him beneath the giant fig trees and others nearer to the massive cedarwood door embellished by oriental carving. The trees had spiky blue flowers that seemed to be at home in the shade of the great arch above the door.

'These are the chaste trees,' said Kharim, somewhat drily. 'Monks' pepper, and supposed to subdue the passions by their coolness and their spikes.'

'Really?' Grace spoke politely, but knew that he was spiking what he considered to be her own lack of passion.

The great cedarwood door stood open and together they

entered the huge tiled hall under the Koranic mosaic of bold carving. Grace saw the half-moon alcoves of the long hall, the blaze of oriental splendour in the tilework and wood-work of the Persian furniture. Overhead the ceiling was aglow with frescoes of the mythical, jewel-tailed phoenix of Persian legend. There was the shimmer of priceless tap-estries, and incense twigs burning in a copper brazier, send-ing up spirals of scented smoke.

What with coming here, and the discovering of her own heart, combined with the incense to put Grace in a rather dazed mood. She was mounting the staircase side by side with the *khan* when all at once she caught her booted foot against one of the marble treads and stumbled. At once he caught hold of her and steadied her, and his touch sent such a discovery of joy through her that instinctively she jerked away from him, before her body obeyed its mad impulse and melted into his arms.

'Don't be so touchy,' he said curtly. 'You stumble and I set you on your feet – what is there to be afraid of in that? Have I not given my word that as soon as time permits I shall ensure your safe return to Reza Shahr? I don't break my word, Lady Wilde.'

'I – I just feel rather tired and nervy,' she stammered. 'This is all so well known to you, but to me it is all very new and strange. I – I'm off balance – it's feeling a solid floor under my feet after the sands of the desert.'

'Quite so,' he agreed. 'Perhaps I am a little touchy as well.'

He led her along a rococo balcony, with lamps hanging above it. Here the walls were bleached to a white silkiness to catch the mountain light through the oval openings, deep and wide enough for a person to sit inside and gaze at moun-tains, sky, and wide-winged hawks.

Here and there were arched doors painted blue, but it wasn't until they rounded the end of the balcony that the *khan* flung open one of these doors and indicated that Grace precede him into the suite of rooms that were revealed. 'I think you will be comfortable here. The door has a large lock, as you can see, and a key so that you can safeguard yourself from me.' The old mocking smile was back in his eyes, and there at the edge of his lips. 'Hathaya my housekeeper will bring you some food after you have bathed, then I suggest that you rest for a few hours. Tonight, if it will please you, you will dine on the roof with me. I should like to make some pretence that we are — amicable. The people of my household are happy to see me home and I don't wish them to sense any discord. By tomorrow certain other tribe leaders will be arriving to have talks with me and you will then be free of much of my company.'

With these words he drew back from the doorway and with sudden oriental gravity he placed fingers against his eyes, lips and heart. 'Until we meet again, *hilwa. Salaam alaykum*.'

He had turned in the corridor abruptly and was gone, leaving that sense of space in the air, echoing with his voice, haunted by his tall robed figure. Very gradually Grace closed her door, in which the great iron-filigreed lock seemed to leer at her. 'Lock me!' it seemed to jeer. 'It won't very much matter, for he won't come seeking you any more. He has found your heart too cold, and your arms like ice sticks beating him away. Kharim Khan is Persian. He is of the desert. He is fierce, but he might have been tender if just once, my lady, you had smiled at him.'

A great lump seemed to rise up in her throat and with a sudden sob Grace ran to the enormous bed, reached by a crescent of steps, and flung herself face down on the thick lace coverlet, to which she clung in her misery, her sense of loss, and new-found empty yearning.

While growing up as her grandfather's ward she had never been allowed the company of boys. Once grown up she had been kept at Jonas' side, an ornament for him to take to the races, to the opera, and the smart houses of the socialites who liked his money. Then had come his announcement that she meet Lord Wilde, and the first open indication that she repay his generosity by agreeing to a marriage in which real love would play no part.

177

Grace quivered against the lace like a creature whipped. She had learned to scorn love in order to protect herself. . . now the love that she so wanted was scorning her.

With a shaky sigh she drew herself upright again, tensed her spine and set her chin. Tomorrow the *khan* would be drawn into tribal discussions with other desert leaders; perhaps for days she would see very little of him. Until this moment she hadn't dreamed how bleak could be the prospect of not seeing that strong brown face, the long stride, and the imperious sweep of the great cloak from the square shoulders. She had only tonight in which to enjoy his company for the last time alone, and it still seemed incredible that she who had feared to be alone with him could now feel this deep longing to be where he was, whether in a desert tent or upon the starlit roof of his palace.

She turned from the bed and saw the soft pile of Eastern garments arranged upon a bedside stool. She took a look at the diaphanous sea-green trousers, the filmy pink shift, and the graceful white silk *haik* to be worn over them. There were finely-wrought silver ornaments laid out on the dressing-table, and upon the carpet stood a pair of silver slippers without heels, made of the softest chamois so they fitted themselves to the foot regardless of size.

Oh no . . . she couldn't possibly wear these things. And yet . . . why not? Her riding boots felt heavy, and there was a grease-mark on her breeches from the breakfast pancake which she had tried to eat in her fingers as neatly as the *khan* ate his.

She stroked the silken shift and allowed the fine material to glide over her arm. She shivered, for the sensation was strangely pleasing. All her life she had worn good clothes, but never had she worn a dress fashioned by Persian fingers, from the silkworms of the Persian mulberry trees. Never had her skin so tingled, nor looked so velvety pale beneath the filmy silk that was the colour of a blush.

Still hesitant, and shy about the garments, Grace decided that if her own things didn't arrive in time for dinner then she would dress herself as a Persian girl.

In the meantime she found a long gown of thick dull silk with enormous sleeves, and this she would wear after taking her bath. She examined her bedroom and the doors leading out of it. She discovered a divan room, with the windows enclosed in one of those iron-laced cages, the floor covered in a huge, soft Kurdistan rug. Grace went across to the caged window and felt as if she trod in the footsteps of one of the *kadins* who would have been kept here by the Khan Rahi, pretty creatures to provide him with pleasure whenever he returned from his forays into the desert.

Grace gazed down upon a secluded courtyard and heard the twittering of birds in the pepper trees and the oleander palms. A lush, orange-petalled honeysuckle lay over the wall of the court, rather like a discarded cloak. And pendulous white lilies watched themselves in the tiled pool.

What, Grace wondered, was it truly like to be a girl kept only for the pleasing of a man? To whom he came in his leisure time, but forgotten, left to wander like a small caged cat when affairs of the desert called him away for months at a time.

A warm finger of sunshine stroked itself across Grace's cheek and felt almost like the fleeting, sympathetic touch of that long-forgotten *kadin*. A scent of trees and flowers wafted up to her, and never before had she felt so alive to all that was lovely and sensuous in nature. Never before had she opened her heart and invited this enslavement of her senses.

What did it matter if she must be hurt when all this beauty was out of her reach, denied to her, as Kharim must be? She would have the memory of this; of those rides across the burning surface of the sands, her scarlet cloak blowing out in unison with the *khan*'s blue cloak, the insignia of his authority, and so much a part of his big graceful body. And never again ... never would she be quite so lonely as she had been ... with Jonas, and with Tony. They had known only the shadow of her. Here she was substance, tormented and aware, and a woman at last.

She slid off the divan and went in search of her bathroom. The tub was a deep one sunken into the tiles of the floor, and turning the taps she let the water run with abandon and tossed into it generous handfuls of the cologne-scented crystals she found in a jar on a tiled shelf. These turned the water blue and emitted a scented cloud, into which Grace soon disappeared, her boots, breeches and shirt flung into a heap on the floor.

The sunken tub was almost large enough to swim about in, and Grace luxuriated in the deep blue water, which felt so good after those jugs of water she had had to make do with in the desert. She closed her eyes and floated, and let the aches and tensions soak out of her limbs. In camp last night she had panicked when Kharim had entered the bathing alcove, and why not? With only a few inches of water in the ewer and most of her pale self out of it!

A smile played over her lips . . . who would have thought it of Grace Tillerton to fall crazily in love with a man of such a different race and upbringing?

And then the smile faded as she remembered that her days at the palace were numbered. Fiercely now she could wish back those first days in the desert, and those nights when she had lain in fear in case he swept aside the curtain of beads and took her by force. She had thought that it was hate she felt, but instead it had been the natural skittish fear of the virgin doe pursued through the forest by the stag, fleeing in circles, until they narrowed and she was caught. But being a chaste woman and not a chased doe she had gone on fighting him, and suddenly he had decided that she wasn't worth the waste of energy. The desire had set like ice in his veins even as her heart had melted.

It was the perverse way of things, and even loving him, she still shrank from being just a woman he made love to and then set aside. It might be heaven to be loved by him . . . but it would be sheerest hell afterwards. '*Au 'voir, madame. Salut, et bonne chance!*' And the offer of a jewel, perhaps.

'No . . .' The word broke from Grace's lips and her face contorted. She would part from him with her pride intact. Ride away from him looking cool, composed, and untouched. He might remember her, then.

She climbed from the bath and wrapped herself in a big towel. As she entered the adjoining bedroom, the door opened and a woman came in. She was an olive-skinned, handsome woman clad in a long plain dress. Her hair was black and intricately arranged, and several rings gleamed on her hands as she placed a tray of food on one of the inlaid tables. She studied Grace with the grave scrutiny encountered in camp from the Persian women; one of interest mingled with a certain perplexity. Grace had wondered several times about that perplexity and had decided that she was considered rather too pale and slender for such a man as the *khan*. She had noticed herself that even Persian girls in their teens were extremely well developed, and had such large, sensuous dark eyes. By contrast, with her slim almost boyish figure *she* looked the teenager.

'I am Hathaya and I keep house for my lord the *khan*.' Abruptly the woman smiled, her white teeth gleaming against her fine olive skin. 'He gives orders that you are to eat the food I bring, and then to put up the feet, as my lady Rachel used to say. But first, *lella*, I will assist you into your robe.'

Hathaya picked up the thick silk robe which Grace had laid ready on the bed and she could not do otherwise than release herself from the big towel and slip her pale body into the folds of the pomegranate-red silk, into which Hathaya proceeded to button her as if she were little more than a child.

'My lady Rachel had a fair enough skin, but you are much fairer, *lella*. Your hair is like sunlight, and perfectly natural. Eh?' Hathaya laughed, and picking up a brush from the dressing-table she proceeded to apply it to Grace's hair. 'Soft, like a small child's. Ah, but you are really not much more than that. Hathaya knows! My lady Rachel taught Hathaya the sensitivity.'

'You—' Grace swallowed a sudden dryness from her throat, 'You keep mentioning the lady Rachel. Who was she, Hathaya?'

'The mother of my lord the *khan*.' Hathaya shot a look at Grace's startled face. 'You did not know? He has not mentioned to you his mother? I wonder why, when he so much loved her? She was extremely wise and clever, and was a writer of books—'

'Books?' Grace exclaimed, and she spun round to stare at Hathaya with a strange premonition thrilling through her body. 'Are you saying the *khan*'s mother was English? Was she by any chance Rachel Leah Bourne, the well-known novelist and travel writer who vanished into the desert all those years ago?'

'That was she.' Hathaya led Grace to the divan beside the table on which she had placed the food. '*Lella*, you are trembling like a sand bird! Come, be seated. You need your food.'

'Hathaya,' Grace caught at the housekeeper's hand, 'I need to be told some more about Rachel Leah Bourne. She truly was the mother of Kharim Khan? She was married to his father? She lived here at the Palace of the Pomegranate?'

'She was the widow of the *khan*'s father.' Now a look of sadness came to Hathaya's vivid face. 'They met in the desert and were married there. But before he could bring her to his palace, there was a military skirmish in which he was gravely injured. My lady and his followers managed to bring him as far as the foot of the mountains, but there he died in her arms. Fortunately the old *khan*, the grandfather of Kharim Khan, was still alive at that time, and he was good to my lady. You see, by then she knew that she was to have a child, and this child, if a boy, would be the heir of the Haklyt Rohim. My lady was persuaded to stay at the palace, and in due time she gave birth to her son. Allah be praised, but what a fine child he was! The old *khan* was beside himself with happiness. Now the people would have their leader. Now the father of Kharim had not died in vain. My lady Rachel became almost a recluse here at the palace. The loss of her husband was always to her a shock from which she never fully recovered. She devoted herself to her son, and tried in no way to make an Englishman of him. She knew that his destiny as *khan* of the Haklyt Rohim must be

182

fulfilled, and that if she attempted to instil into him the ways of her own people he might rebel against the life that lay ahead of him, a strict devotion and loyalty to his tribe; to their ways, their mode of life, their right to expect his protection and his affection.'

Hathaya paused and spread her hands in a very Eastern way. 'Since my lady died, when Kharim Khan was seventeen years of age, he has devoted himself to his tribe. When I heard that he had brought with him to the palace an English girl I, for one, was unsurprised. No matter how much of him is Persian from his father, and all the long line of *khans,* he is still his mother's son. She gave birth to him, and she loved him with all her heart, and so it is inevitable that he will have eyes for an English woman and see in her a little of his mother, and hear in her voice an echo of his mother's voice. He is only human!'

Grace had listened to all this in a kind of spell. It seemed unbelievable, and yet having known a little of the desert she could now believe what desert people said of life. That it was *mektub.* Spelled out in the stars and impossible to escape.

Her course to the Palace of the Pomegranate had been set from the moment she had read Rachel Leah Bourne's book about the desert and been drawn to discovering for herself the Garden of Sheba. Now she knew what the garden signified . . . it was the place where a woman found a love beyond any other kind of love. Rachel had found that love, and then in grief had lost it, and like a true Persian widow of legend she had gone into *purdah* and had not emerged again to become a member of her own world. She had ceased to write, and had lived only for her son, until she died and was reunited with her husband.

As a story it was wonderful . . . .as a reality it still left Grace gasping, and so dry-throated that she finished her jasmine tea at a gulp and held out the cup for more. Hathaya poured it, and coaxed her to eat the veal cutlets and rice, with baby marrows and beans in a sauce with a delectable aroma.

'You have journeyed in the desert and this can be trying for those who are unaccustomed to the heat and hardship. Please, *lella*, so that I will be able to take back to the kitchen an empty plate and not have to furnish my lord with a lie. He said I was to bully you until you ate, but I find it difficult to be stern with someone so young, so fair, who speaks as my lady spoke.'

'You're kind, Hathaya, and just to please you I will eat my lunch.' Grace picked up a fork and tried a few mouthfuls of rice. It was delicious and sparked off the appetite which had lain dormant in her since her arrival at the palace. She had felt such a stranger, shy and afraid of the love she had discovered in herself, but now she learned that for almost eighteen years another woman of English blood had walked these halls, had lived here and loved the place. Now she knew why the books of Rachel Leah Bourne travelled in the camel-wraps of Kharim Khan. His mother! About whom he might have spoken if Grace had been a little more forthcoming.

'You have a family, Hathaya?'

'I have three sons, *lella*. Davoud, my eldest son, is *aide-de-camp* to the *khan*, and you perhaps know him?'

'Why, of course! He's very good-looking and very charming.'

'Indeed so.' But Hathaya pursed her lips as she spoke. 'He knows he has such charm and he keeps waiting his young fiancée while he struts and smiles for other girls. The trouble is — I don't think he will marry until my lord Kharim takes a wife. They grew up together, you see, *lella*. Almost they have been as brothers, riding, hawking, fighting in the desert. Until one settles the other will not.'

'So the *khan* has no wife?' Grace had been unsure until this moment, for as a Persian the *khan* was entitled to four wives, and as a prince there had been every chance that he was married . . . if not from love, then in order to provide an heir to his title and his duties.

'It does not please certain elders of the tribe that he refrains from marriage,' Hathaya's white teeth flashed a wicked smile, 'but when he was a boy and a betrothal would have been arranged for him with a young cousin of the tribe, my lady Rachel opposed such a betrothal. She said that as the tribe would have her son in almost everything, it was only fair that he be allowed to be English in just this one small matter, that he choose his own wife when he was ready to do so. Surprisingly the old *khan* backed her in this, and though there was grumbling in the tribe, it became an accepted fact that Kharim be granted the freedom to marry when the will took him.

'I wonder,' Hathaya picked up the diaphanous Eastern garments Grace would have to wear later on if her own clothes did not arrive before nightfall, 'when the will to wed will take strong hold of our young, strong and handsome *khan*? He is much of a man, eh, *lella*? A stallion who has trodden his wild oats and must soon settle down with a wife.'

'He is allowed four wives, I understand.' Grace had finished her main course and had started on her sweet yoghourt to which slices of apricot had been added.

'He will not lumber himself with four wives.' Hathaya broke into laughter at the idea. 'Very few Persians do so, these days. Any man will say that one wife is enough to cope with, especially if that man is kept as busy as the *khan*. Added to which he has much of his mother in him, and she loved but one man until the day she died. She loved the *khan*'s father greatly and hardly knew after she lost him that other men existed. Her blood, her emotions, and inclinations run also in Kharim Khan, and we have a saying that the wolf cannot change its mask.'

Suddenly Hathaya was looking closely at Grace, searching her rather pensive face as she leaned back against the cushions of the divan, her meal finished and her hunger satisfied.

'My young lady has something eating at her heart,' Hathaya murmured. 'Is it the love which she feels for my lord?'

Grace glanced with shocked eyes at Hathaya. Oh no, it

couldn't show so plainly . . . she wouldn't be able to face him again if love had so unmasked her face.

'The *lella* must not mind if I guess her secret.' Hathaya gathered up the tray in readiness to take it away, and her smile was kind. 'Be proud of it, for it is a supreme gift to be able to give one's heart, and when it happens for the first time it is always overwhelming.'

'Don't you know that I am a widow, Hathaya? That my husband died in the desert?'

'I know of this – but I know also that the *lella* did not bury her heart in the desert but brought it with her to the palace. Why, my child, would you care if the *khan* had four wives and forty concubines – if you did not care for him? And now I will take away the tray and you will rest – put up the feet, eh?'

Grace looked at Hathaya with large, gravely blue eyes, and then she smiled slowly. 'I think you are a witch, Hathaya.'

'I think you are right, *lella*, but that also we will keep a secret.'

The door closed behind the Persian woman, and after a minute or so Grace allowed herself to relax among the divan cushions. There was silence beyond the windows as if the birds were also drowsy, and in a while she closed her eyes and her cheek sank against a tawny silk cushion and she slept.

Twilight had crept into the bedroom when Grace awoke from her deep and refreshing sleep. She stretched and eased her curled-up limbs, and when her eyes became accustomed to the gloom she roused herself completely and climbed to her feet.

There was a blue-shaded kerosene lamp on the dressing-table and beside it a box of matches, and when she had lit the lamp Grace saw her face reflected in the mirror, all eyes and cheekbones and lips softened by sleep. The high satin collar of her deep red robe stood up about her face and she saw there the innocence which Hathaya had seen. The blue eyes that wondered, and the lips that were poignant as a lonely flower against the smooth paleness of her skin.

During those days of desert riding she had swathed her face in the muslin *shesh*, not from vanity but because the *khan* had ordered it, on account of her fairness, and the cruelty of the sun. He had said that her skin would blister if she wasn't careful, and as she recalled her reply to him she pressed her hands to her cheeks and felt them burn.

'Won't you want me, my lord, if I'm blistered and hideous?' she had asked.

What a little shrew she had been at times . . . but she didn't want to be remembered by him as a shrew. She wanted . . . oh yes, she knew what she wanted. To be again the girl he had seen in that Persian garden; a girl not yet embittered by a loveless marriage, who had listened wide-eyed as a singer among the trees sang of the forces of destiny.

When she turned from the mirror she saw that while she slept someone had come into the room very quietly and placed her suitcases on a carved chest that stood against the wall. She gnawed her lip and knew that she had a choice now between wearing a dinner dress of her own, or the filmy Persian trousers and shift, and the silken *haik* that was a kind of top-to-toe veil.

Her heart beat fast and the old inhibitory shyness was at odds with her desire to play the *kadin*, this one and only night of her life. In the lamplight the silver slippers embroidered with pearls glimmered and beckoned. She would try them . . . yes, like Cinderella she would try the silver slippers, and if they fitted her . . . a smile trembled on her lips . . . somehow she knew that they would fit her.

By the time Grace had dressed herself, darkness had crept over the gardens and courts of the palace and the stars were beginning to sparkle in the sky. She went to the balcony and breathed the perfume of the jasmine, which like the stars was more alive at night then during the heat of the day.

It was a 'night of nights' as the Eastern people said, with the air as soft and tangible as fine silk, brushing against the skin, scented and sensuous.

Grace had not yet dared to look at herself in the mirror; she was afraid that she might see a caricature of a Persian girl. A masquerade figure the *khan* would only laugh at. The little enamelled clock under the glass dome made a sudden chiming sound and all her nerves were so on edge that her heart seemed to turn over. Any minute now a servant would come to escort her to the *khan*, and suddenly she felt that she couldn't face him in these harem trousers, and the silky veil that billowed around her as she flew to the mirror and looked at herself.

Her hair was loose but for the *chand bina*, and her skin had the glimmer of fine porcelain under the Persian silk. She was instantly petrified by her own appearance ... she was like a beautiful, wanton butterfly, and even as she knew that she couldn't go to him like this, a tap came at the door, and as it opened she whirled to say to the servant that she wasn't ready to go and meet the *khan*.

But it was the *khan* who entered ... and to her utter amazement he was wearing European dress-suit, dark and formal and perfectly tailored, with a white shirt-front that gleamed against the dark material. His black hair was well groomed above his bronzed face ... and the instant they looked at each other they exclaimed in unison: 'Oh no!' her cry in English blended with his: 'I don't believe it!'

They stood there, eyes locked, and then a smile began to quirk at the corner of his lips.

'That's right,' she stormed, 'go ahead and laugh at the ridiculous figure of fun I've made of myself!'

'But you aren't ridiculous, not for one moment.'

'Then why are you smiling in that way?'

'Well, is it not amusing that I should wear this sober suit from Savile Row, and find you looking like a piece of Persian delight?' As he spoke he glanced casually around the room, and Grace saw his eyes rest upon her suitcases. 'I thought they had been brought to you, then why—?'

'I – I was just seeing how I would look. It won't take me more than a few minutes to change—'

'I would not think of it.' Suddenly he came to her and took hold of her by the hands, and feeling them quiver nervously he glanced down at them, pale and slim within his own brown hands. 'I would have you dine with me just as you are.'

'So that I can amuse you?' She struggled to release her hands from his, but it was useless. 'Y-you're hurting me!'

'You are hurting yourself, so stop it.'

'I wish you'd stop dictating to me!'

'Do you?' There was a deep purring sound to his voice. 'Shall we now go to the roof, where I like to eat dinner on a fine night. Tonight is exceptionally fine, so you will not feel cold in these filmy fabrics.'

Holding her by the hand, he led her firmly from the room, so that her silks brushed against the smooth darkness of his suit, in which he looked leaner than in his robes, his length of leg intensified, and the contrast between his green eyes and his proud Persian features no longer the mystery they had been.

Suddenly it rushed over Grace that she loved him, and had found out that love before Hathaya had told her about his mother. As they mounted a twisting iron stairway to the rooftop and the stars, she felt a compulsion to speak of Rachel, but a shyness gripped her throat and there upon the roof she could only stand by the parapet of star-washed stone and gaze silently at the mountains above them, and the miles of sand below them. A silver ocean, so peaceful right now, so cool and chaste.

Here, she thought, his mother had often sat and gazed at the desert . . . the desert where she had found love, and lost it.

Beside her at the parapet the *khan* stood tall and silent, and Grace knew that he, too, was thinking of Rachel. His hand rested close to hers, she had only to move her fingers and she would touch him . . . and if she did so, he would mock her, for only a short while ago she had resisted his touch . . . resisted as if it burned her when all the time it thrilled her.

She stirred to a sudden restlessness and her gaze followed the glowing flight of the night moths, and the pale glimmer of the moonflower vines trained over the wall of the tower.

The soft night wind fluttered her long, nun-like cloak, so in contrast to the filmy garments beneath it. She was slender and ivory-pale as she stood there, unaware of her own youthful grace . . . unaware that the stars revealed her eyes. Oh, this night of a soft dense beauty littered with stars . . . how it turned the heart over and over as she looked blindly at Kharim, up into his darkly brooding, almost stern face.

They looked at each other, a man and a woman alone together . . . they looked, and then like a star bursting into stunning silver pieces the truth struck at them. It was a moment drawn out into what seemed an eternity, holding what could never be forgotten . . . the raw blaze of love in the jade-green eyes . . . the melting sublimaton in the blue eyes made naked by the stars.

The incandescence of the truth lit them in its light, and then he reached for her, savage and exultant as his mouth crushed hers, and his arms shackled her to him, a pain and a pleasure that shot through her body like a flame.

He had been born of an English mother, but in his heart and his bones he was a Persian, of a different creed and culture . . . yet Grace knew as he held her that they were one heart, one soul, mingling for ever in their two bodies.

He was Persian, a tribal *khan* with immense responsibilities, but he was the man who loved her as no one of her own race had ever loved her. She knew, held close in his arms, kissed until the heavens whirled around her, that he would defy Persian convention and make her his wife, taking unto himself a bride of his heart, as Rachel had desired.

Somewhere in a Persian garden a man had sung of destiny . . . and here on the tower of a Persian palace Grace Tillerton came home to her destiny . . . and it was glorious.

**Mills & Boon Classics**

The very best of Mills & Boon
romances, brought back for those of you
who missed reading them when they
were first published.

There are three other Classics for you to collect this
October

### NO QUARTER ASKED
*by Janet Dailey*

Stacy Adams was a rich girl who wanted to sample real life for
a change, so she courageously took herself off alone to Texas
for a while. It was obvious from the first that the arrogant
rancher Cord Harris, for some reason, disapproved of her — but
why should she care what he thought?

### MIRANDA'S MARRIAGE
*by Margery Hilton*

Desperation forced Miranda to encamp for the night in Jason
Steele's office suite, but unfortunately he found her there, and
after the unholy wrath that resulted she never dreamed that a
few months later she would become his wife. For Jason was
reputed to be a rake where women were concerned. So what
chance of happiness had Miranda?

### THE LIBRARY TREE
*by Lilian Peake*

Carolyn Lyle was the niece of a very influential man, and
nothing would convince her new boss, that iceberg Richard
Hindon, that she was nothing but a spoiled, pampered darling
who couldn't be got rid of fast enough! Had she even got time
to make him change his mind about her?

If you have difficulty in obtaining any of these books through
your local paperback retailer, write to:

**Mills & Boon Reader Service**
**P.O. Box 236, Thornton Road, Croydon, Surrey, CR9 3RU.**

# Give yourself and your friends a romantic Christmas.

First time in paperback, four superb romances
by favourite authors, in an attractive maroon and
gold gift pack. A superb present to give. And to receive.

**Sandstorm**
Anne Mather

**Man's World**
Charlotte Lamb

**Lord of the High Valley**
Margaret Way

**Enemy In Camp**
Janet Dailey

| United Kingdom | £2.60 |
| Rep. of Ireland | £2.86 |
| Publication | 10th October 1980 |

Look for this gift pack at your local Mills & Boon stockist.

 **The Mills & Boon rose is the rose of romance**